THE LACE AND THE LIE

A SLOW BURN FANTASY ROMANCE OF ROYAL
BETRAYAL, FORBIDDEN MAGIC, AND A WARRIOR
WHO CANNOT CHOOSE DUTY OVER LOVE

THE LOOM OF OATH AND EMBER
BOOK ONE

LIORA M VALEN

CONTENTS

1

Mira Nerielle liked silence. The royal atelier was rarely quiet, but she knew how to carve a small piece of quiet for herself even in a room full of people. Ever since she started working here, she had learned how to take up as little space as possible. No one expected conversation from her, and she gave them nothing more than what her work required. Her hands were busy. That was enough.

The morning sun filtered through the tall glass windows, catching on a long embroidered sleeve spread carefully across her lap. Pearls reflected bits of light against her dark hair and pale fingers. She stitched with even, gentle movements, guiding the needle without hurry. She needed to fix a tear hardly larger than the width of her thumb. A noblewoman had returned the garment in outrage, claiming she could feel the flaw even if she could barely see it. Mira hid a small shake of her head and focused on the thread.

Her magic hummed under her skin, a quiet warmth in the center of her palm. She let the warmth rise only a little, the way she might allow a soft breath. If she opened too wide, the magic would affect the entire garment. If she closed it completely, the stitching would be ordinary thread and nothing more. She needed it to be seamless, stronger than before but not noticeably altered. She sent a small pulse into the thread, just enough to reinforce the weakened fabric.

No one watching would think she did anything unusual. Her needle moved. The tear closed. The pearls and silk lay smooth again.

When she was finished, she cut her final stitch and set the sleeve down lightly. The head tailor, Mistress Varani, had her back turned across the room, barking instructions at two apprentices who were always late with their fabric inventory. Mira took advantage of the moment to rest her hands. The tiny tremor that followed any use of magic faded slowly. She rubbed her fingertips together to settle it.

"Well done," whispered a voice near her shoulder.

Liron, a journeyman tailor a few years older than Mira, leaned closer to look at the repaired sleeve. He had a round face, quick eyes and a tendency to whisper gossip while working. He respected Mira, though he never understood her quietness.

"It looks untouched," he murmured. "Not even Mistress Varani will notice where the tear was."

Mira allowed the smallest smile. "That is the idea."

"You should be proud. Half the staff here wants to be noticed for their work. You hide yours like a secret." Liron shook his head and reached for a pile of wool coats that needed lining. "You would think someone would want praise. Just once."

Praise makes you remembered. Mira did not say it. She did not need anyone remembering what she could do. She took pride in her work, but she had never wanted attention for it. The type of attention her skill might bring was dangerous. Skills like hers could be used, controlled, owned.

She folded the sleeve into a sheet of tissue paper and slid it into a waiting box. The morning moved on. She reached for the next piece, a delicate shawl of sheer gold threading, when the heavy double doors swung open.

They struck the wall loud enough to silence the entire room at once. Every needle stopped. Even Mistress Varani halted her scolding and turned, a stiff look of irritation crossing her sharp face.

A man dressed in the deep red of the royal court stood in the doorway. His uniform bore a silver insignia at the chest, the mark of a royal messenger. His dark hair was tied neatly back, and his posture demanded attention with no words at all. He looked over the room full of tailors, garment menders, designers and embroiderers with a slow sweep of his eyes, taking stock of everyone present.

Mira lowered her gaze to the shawl in her hands without actually working. She knew better than to draw curiosity. She let her shoulders round slightly and tried to disappear into the chair.

The messenger stepped forward. His boots clicked against the marble floor with the sharp, confident rhythm of someone used to being obeyed.

"By decree of Her Highness, Princess Selene of Varyn," he announced, voice deep and formal, "a new royal commission is required."

A ripple of interest passed through the room. A royal commission meant prestige and competition. Even Mistress Varani gave a small incline of her head to show respect.

The messenger lifted a rolled scroll sealed with a violet ribbon. He broke the seal and read aloud.

"The princess seeks an artisan to design and construct ceremonial attire for a binding rite to be held this season. Embellishment of protection is required. Secrecy required. All aspects of the commission shall remain known only to the artisan selected. Punishable by decree if violated."

The room went completely still. Everyone understood what that meant. A job this important could elevate someone for the rest of their life. It could also ruin them if they made a mistake. The palace did not tolerate failure lightly. Royal garments were not just clothing. They were symbols of power, identity, and sometimes, magical rite.

Mistress Varani stepped forward with a graceful bow. "Your Highness honors the atelier with such a request. I will select our most capable tailor for this task. I assure you we will—"

The messenger raised a gloved hand without looking at her. His gesture was not rude, but it cut her speech in half. Murmurs broke out among the apprentices. Varani stiffened. Mira felt a tightness gather in her throat. Something was wrong. The head tailor always chose who received royal commissions. The crown did not interfere in such matters. Until now.

"The selection has already been made," the messenger said.

The room was quiet again. Mira kept her eyes on the shawl, though her heart pulsed harder. She had done nothing to put herself forward. She never would.

The messenger scanned the workers, looking past those who clearly wanted his attention. People straightened, trying to look dignified or skilled without appearing desperate. Mira knew this dance well. She stayed still.

His gaze reached her. He stopped.

"You. Seamstress Mira Nerielle."

It took a heartbeat for the name to register. Liron's breath caught beside her. His eyes shot wide. Several workers whispered. Mistress Varani stiffened even further, face tense with surprise and irritation. Mira rose slowly from her chair, unsure if her legs would hold her.

She had never spoken higher than a greeting to the noble messengers. She had never designed anything for royalty. She was one of the invisible ones, valued for precision, not recognition.

The messenger spoke again. "Your presence is suitable to the commission. You are precise. You are quiet. You are discreet. That is what is required."

The words did not feel like praise. They were descriptions. She was chosen not because she was exceptional or talented, but because she was forgettable. Someone who would not talk. Someone who would not cause trouble. Someone who could be hidden while doing important work.

"I am honored," Mira said. She did not know what else one was supposed to say. Her voice sounded small, but steady. The messenger nodded once.

"You will be bound to secrecy by oath. Designs, materials, enchantment requests, measurement sessions, and all progress must remain confidential. Do you accept these terms, Seamstress Nerielle?"

There was no way to refuse without consequence. Refusal would show suspicion. It would label her uncooperative. It might even be treasonous to refuse a royal oath.

"I accept," she answered.

The messenger's posture eased just slightly, as though a box in his duties had been checked. He continued reading from the scroll with a ceremonial tone.

"Then let the artisan know the commission. You will design the ceremonial wedding attire for Commander Kael Ardyn."

Several gasps escaped before anyone could stop them.

Kael Ardyn. The First Blade of the Crown. The general who had ended the last border conflict in a single decisive campaign. He was a man whispered about in barracks, taverns and war stories. Some said he had saved the kingdom twice over. Others said he had spilled so much blood that even the gods turned their faces from him. Everyone knew his name.

The princess was marrying him.

Mira's breath stalled. Her pulse raced without permission. Commander Kael was more myth than man, yet she had seen him before. Not in passing at a parade. Not in full armor across a battlefield. She had been close enough to see his skin pale with blood loss. Close enough to touch him. Close enough to save him.

The messenger did not notice her reaction. He gave the formal closing line.

"The Commander will arrive for fitting within the week. Have materials prepared and workspace secured. The crown thanks you for your service."

He bowed slightly. Mistress Varani returned the gesture, though her expression was tight and dissatisfied. As he left through the wide doors, the atelier erupted into whispers.

"No one chooses an unknown for a royal garment."

"They must want someone they can control."

"Commander Kael requires enchantments. This is dangerous work."

"She is too quiet. She will not survive this secret."

Mira sat as soon as she could reach her chair. Her hands trembled slightly. She placed them in her lap, pretending to smooth out her skirt so no one would notice.

Liron leaned toward her with eyes full of both excitement and warning. "Mira, you cannot refuse now. But this is not safe."

She kept her gaze on her hands. "I know."

"They will expect perfection, and more than that. Royal cloth is a symbol. With rituals involved who knows what kind of enchantments they expect." He lowered his voice even further. "If they find out what you can do without asking for it, they might make you do it on command."

The words stung because they were true. She had always feared being pushed into someone else's control. She had magic she barely understood. She kept it quiet because she did not know how far it reached or what mistakes she could make with it. Magic bound things. It strengthened them. Sometimes it did more. She did not want to find out what would happen if someone demanded she push it further.

Mistress Varani approached. Mira straightened instinctively, trying to appear composed. Varani's expression was a strange mix of resentment and forced professionalism.

"You will be given a private workspace," Varani said. "By order of the crown. I do not approve, but I have no choice." She paused, lips pressed tightly. "Understand that if you fail, it reflects on this atelier. Keep whatever talent you have under control. This is not a performance. It is a duty."

"Yes, Mistress."

"And remember, this opportunity is not a gift. It is a test. The palace will judge you harshly. Do not disappoint us."

Varani left before Mira could respond.

The day moved painfully slow after that. Everyone watched Mira from the corner of their eyes. Some jealousy, some sympathy, and some fear. When the midday bell rang, Mira barely tasted her meal. Her stomach felt like a stone, heavy and unsettled. Work continued through the afternoon, but her attention wandered in moments that normally would have kept her fully focused. She finished two more garments, both ordinary repairs, nothing that required her magic. That was a relief. She could barely breathe, much less control her abilities with precision.

At the end of the day, she left the atelier with the rest of the workers, but she felt separated from them, as though the moment she was chosen, she had stopped belonging to the group. She walked through the palace servant halls, quiet and plain, made of cold stone with narrow windows. A few workers nodded to her, still whispering about her new responsibility. She kept her eyes lowered and hurried outside.

Mira lived in the small servant district behind the palace grounds. It was a cluster of modest houses with thin walls and simple gardens, nothing elegant but cleaner and safer than most city neighborhoods. She rented a single room at the top floor of a narrow gray building. It held a tiny bed, a cracked mirror, a wooden chest for clothes and a single narrow window that overlooked the palace wall.

The moment she closed the door behind her, she exhaled with all the quiet desperation she had held back all day. She set her sewing satchel on the floor and sank onto the bed. For a long time, she only listened to her heartbeat, trying to let it slow.

Commander Kael. She would be making clothing for a man she had once saved at the edge of death. She had kept that moment hidden, never telling anyone that she had slipped into a battlefield camp a year and a half ago. She had been traveling with her cousin to deliver supplies to a wounded regiment. The commander had been there, pale and unconscious, with healers struggling to keep him alive.

She remembered kneeling beside him, pretending to adjust his blanket so she could touch his skin. She had pushed magic into him, unsure if it would heal, unsure if it would do anything helpful. She had felt a surge of warmth spread through him. His breathing had steadied. She had left before anyone saw her. She had never expected to see him again.

Now she would stand in front of him. He would speak to her. He would wear something she created. Something she shaped with her hands and her magic. She felt a small tremor of fear in her fingertips again. She pressed them against the mattress to stop the shaking.

She was not ready. Not for him. Not for the princess. Not for royal secrets and ritual magic. Not for whatever binding rite she had promised to help create. But there was no way to refuse. She had accepted. She had spoken the oath publicly. The crown had chosen someone quiet because that person could not fight back. Mira closed her eyes.

Outside her window, the palace loomed in the twilight. Lanterns lit the stone walls with a faint amber glow. The night air was cool and smelled faintly of smoke from faraway hearths. She felt hollow, as though someone had scooped out the space behind her ribs and left only weight.

She whispered into the quiet room, "What have I done."

Her hands, resting in her lap, warmed again. The magic in her body responded to her unsettled thoughts, reaching toward something she could not see, something it remembered. She clenched her fists slowly until the warmth faded again. She needed to control it. She needed to stay invisible, quiet, discreet. She needed to survive this.

Her life had changed in a single moment. She could not undo it. The garment she would make for Commander Kael would be more than silk and thread. It would be a bond. A risk. A secret.

And she was the one chosen to weave it.

2

The palace smelled like polished stone and cold metal. It always did, but Mira had never noticed the scent quite this sharply. She walked through the inner hall beside a palace steward, a neat woman with a strict expression and a clipboard tucked to her chest. The woman's name was Iris Merrow. Mira had heard her name many times. Iris oversaw artisans with a severity that often left apprentices shaking.

"Keep up," Iris said without raising her voice. Mira took a longer step to match her stride.

They walked past a series of tall doors, each carved with flowers and beasts that symbolized different branches of the royal family. Mira had passed these doors before while returning finished garments, but she had never been permitted beyond the common work floor. Now she walked deeper. Servants in navy uniforms moved out of the way as Iris approached. The steward did not slow or acknowledge anyone unless they spoke directly to her. Mira felt smaller with every step.

The hall narrowed ahead, then widened into a secluded corridor lined with portraits of past rulers. Iris stopped at a wooden door near the end, its handle shaped like a twisting branch. She removed a small key from her belt.

"This will be your workspace until your commission is complete," Iris said. She unlocked the door and held it open. "Remember, privacy is a privilege. Do not make the kingdom regret granting it to you."

Mira stepped inside. The room was larger than she expected, not luxurious but well supplied. A wide table dominated the space. It held bolts of untouched silk, spools of thread, and brushes for dye work. A simple stool sat beside it, waiting for her. A tapestry loom stood against the far wall, unused. A mannequin rested in the corner, shaped to a male frame. Mira did not look too closely at it yet.

She swallowed the uneasy feeling in her throat. This room would become her world for weeks.

Iris closed the door behind them and continued speaking, her tone clipped. "All materials here are recorded. You are responsible for their use and condition. Any alteration you make must be intentional and documented. You will not leave this workspace while you are working, unless summoned or dismissed. Meals will be delivered. Personal breaks will be brief. Understood?"

Mira nodded. "Yes, Steward Merrow."

Iris studied her for a moment. "You will not get special treatment. You will be observed without appearing to be observed. Many commissions have crushed artisans before you. Remember that if you start feeling bold."

Mira did not think she would ever feel bold here, especially not with the weight of what she carried. "I understand."

Iris set her clipboard on the table. She placed two documents in front of Mira. One was a seam map for ceremonial attire. The other was a single-page contract written in dense script. Mira read the first lines. She was forbidden to speak, sketch or display any part of the project outside this room. Only the steward and royal tailors with clearance could view her progress. Violation meant punishment ranging from imprisonment to removal of privileges. Removal of privileges could mean anything. Even the right to use her hands.

Mira lifted her eyes to Iris. "I will follow every rule."

Iris did not smile. She simply nodded once and left the room. The door clicked shut.

Silence followed. Mira looked at her future.

She touched the table lightly. Her fingers traced the smooth edge as though testing if it would disappear beneath her hand. The silk bolts gleamed faintly in the light from the high window. Some were white so pale they looked silver. Others held a soft blue tint like moonlight on water. There were threads of beaten gold, but not too bright, not flashy. Nothing in this room was meant for vanity. Ritual garments were something else entirely.

Mira pulled the seam map closer, flattening it on the table. It showed diagrams of sleeves, hems and lining. A garment of protection. A garment for a binding. The symbols etched along the collar area resembled ancient characters. She recognized a few. They were common in oath ceremonies. They marked allegiance, identity and sacrifice. Her stomach tightened.

She opened the materials ledger, noting exactly what was provided. Silk from the northern orchards, known for strength under enchantment. Gold thread from the palace reserves, rarely used without purpose. Needles hammered from iron softened by salt water. She felt a faint pulse in her fingers, the same whisper of warmth that reacted whenever she touched a tool meant to carry power.

She took a slow breath. She needed to begin.

Mira smoothed a sheet of parchment next to the seam map and set a fresh quill. She dipped the quill into ink and wrote a heading.

Ceremonial attire: Commander Kael Ardyn

Her hand paused over the name. The ink glistened in the light. She had never written his name before. She remembered the night she had saved him. She had not known his name then. She only knew the rumors, the same rumors that made people fear him now. The same fear she carried because she had touched him and seen a different truth.

She set the quill down. She picked up a bolt of fabric and held it against her palms. The silk felt smooth and cool, like river water. She measured a length with her arm and cut carefully. The scissors slid through the silk with a clean, satisfying sound.

Her magic stirred. The fabric awakened slightly under her fingers, sensing her intention. She closed her eyes and pressed her hand flat to the table, letting her pulse settle.

The door opened again. She turned quickly.

It was Iris Merrow. She stepped inside with a tray of tea and left it on a small side table. "Before you begin," Iris said, "there is something you should hear from someone who has worked here long enough to know how dangerous this type of commission is."

Mira straightened. The steward looked at her with an expression Mira could not read.

"You may think the greatest risk in this work is detail. It is not. It is compliance. Do exactly as instructed. The palace does not like creativity in matters of ritual. Do not improve anything that has not been ordered. Do not allow your skill to dictate the design. It will tempt you. Resist it."

Mira understood at once. The palace feared magic that was not theirs. She nodded. "Yes, Steward. I will not change anything."

Iris studied her for another moment. "There are rumors about Commander Kael. You will hear more of them. Ignore them. You are here to work. Not to know him. Not to judge him."

Mira kept her voice quiet. "I understand."

Iris hesitated. She lowered her voice for the first time. "You are not here because you are the best. You are here because you are unlikely to speak of what you see. They believe they can trust you. Do not break that trust. It will not go well for you."

She left again. The door shut with a soft click.

Mira did not move for a long moment. The tea on the tray released a faint scent of mint. She tried to breathe it in, but it did not calm her.

A knuckle rapped on the door frame. She turned again. A palace guard stood there. He was older, with stern lines around his mouth and a scar under his eye.

"Seamstress," he said. "The Commander's regiment will patrol through the eastern courtyard today. You are advised to stay inside during that time."

She frowned slightly. "Why would I need to?"

The guard clasped his hands behind his back. "People sometimes forget to keep quiet when they see him. They forget the boundaries. They regret it."

Mira felt a faint chill on her arms. "Is he dangerous?"

The guard only held her gaze. "He is a weapon. Weapons are not judged for danger. They are judged for use."

He turned and walked away.

Mira watched him go, confused yet unsettled. She closed the door gently and rested her hand against the wood. The palace feared their own general. That fear flowed through the walls, lingering in servants' voices and stewards' warnings. They spoke about him as if he were not a man, but a storm that could strike anyone without reason.

She did not see a storm when she had saved him. She had seen someone fighting to breathe.

Mira returned to the table and forced herself to focus. She cut more silk, measured collar lengths and prepared the threads. Hours blurred into careful work. The tea grew cold without her noticing. She marked the patterns for protective seams, leaving room for the enchantments she would have to place later. She worked steadily, but her mind drifted often to how she would manage her magic without drawing attention. She needed just enough to reinforce the garment, no more. If she overstepped, the cloth would reveal her.

One mistake could expose her ability. One exposure could strip her freedom.

The door opened again. She looked up, startled.

Two servants entered, carrying boxes of supplies. They opened them on the floor without her direction, as though trained for this. One of them, a young woman with freckles, looked up briefly and whispered to her coworker. Mira caught the words.

"I hope she knows what he is. They say he lost control once and killed his own men."

The other servant shushed her quickly. "Not here."

The rumor hung in the air anyway. Mira felt the tension tighten in her shoulders.

When the servants left, the room seemed colder. She rubbed her arms, though she was not cold. She knew rumors could twist truth. People build monsters out of mystery. But she could not deny what she remembered. When she had saved him, he had been covered in blood. Most of it was not his. He had looked like someone who did not know how to stop fighting, even on a weak breath.

The hours passed. Mira kept working until her hands ached with repetition. When Iris checked in again, she inspected the progress without comment. She only nodded and left. That was the closest thing to praise Mira expected.

Late afternoon light shifted into early evening. Mira had completed enough preparations to begin stitching the outer layer. She cleaned her tools and organized the table so it would be ready. She brushed loose threads from her skirt. Her shoulders were tense and sore.

A palace bell sounded in the distance. Voices echoed faintly from the hall. Footsteps gathered outside. A murmur spread like a current.

Someone important was approaching.

Mira's breath caught. She looked at the door.

The door handle turned.

She straightened her posture without meaning to. Her heart beat hard in her chest. The fabric beneath her palms felt almost alive, responding to the presence approaching from outside.

A voice spoke just beyond the doorway. Firm, low, quiet. She recognized it before she saw him.

She had heard it once, barely conscious, when he tried to speak through blood.

Commander Kael Ardyn had arrived.

3

Mira did not see Commander Kael again that day. He did not enter the workroom despite his presence outside the door, and the moment passed as quickly as it arrived. Guards spoke to him briefly. He moved on, and the palace returned to its routines. Mira did not know if she felt relieved or disappointed. It was easier not to think about that question.

The following morning began with a knock that came too early. Mira rose from her narrow bed and dressed quietly, forcing her thoughts into stillness. She tied her hair back with a simple ribbon and slipped her sewing satchel over her shoulder. Dawn light barely touched the sky outside her window. She walked back to the palace while the city remained a breath away from waking.

When she entered the atelier hallway, Iris Merrow was waiting with her usual rigid posture. She held a sealed folder that looked heavier than paper ought to.

"You will meet with Princess Selene shortly," Iris said without greeting. "She wants to speak about the garment's enchantment requirements. She will expect questions, but only ones that help you complete the work. You are not there to discuss rumors, personal matters or court politics."

Mira nodded. "I understand."

"Do not speak unless she directly asks you to. Do not volunteer opinions that have not been requested."

Mira nodded again. Iris studied her face, as if trying to measure how likely she was to disobey.

"I hope you do," Iris said. "Because if you misstep, it will not be the princess who suffers consequences. It will be the artisan who acted beyond her role."

She handed Mira the sealed folder. "These are pattern drafts and ceremonial notes. Study them before you are called inside."

Mira held the folder close as Iris led her to a waiting room furnished with low chairs and a narrow table bearing a silver pitcher of water. The room was quiet, and a single tall curtain filtered morning light across the floor. Iris instructed her to stay seated until summoned, then left without any further words.

Mira sat and opened the folder carefully. The first pages contained diagrams similar to the seam map she had already seen, but behind them lay handwritten notes. She turned page after page, absorbing every line. Some details concerned color symbolism, others marked where protection should be focused on the garment. The largest amount of emphasis surrounded the chest, wrists and throat.

A short paragraph near the end caught her attention.

The binding rite must be facilitated with ceremonial cloth, without external spellcasters present. All enchantment signatures must belong solely to the artisan of the garment.

Mira read it twice. The enchantment would not be assisted or controlled by court mages. The garment alone would carry the magic. That meant her stitching would act in the place of a trained caster. She felt her pulse rise slowly into her throat.

Another note described materials used in ancient rites. Gold thread, water tempered iron, silk from orchards blessed by the first royal line. All of that was manageable. Then she found one more detail in a small margin of script.

In the final hour, the wearer's blood must touch the cloth.

Mira froze, breath caught halfway between inhale and exhale. She stared at the line again, afraid she had misread it.

Blood. Ritual garments required contact with the wearer's blood. Why did no one warn her more clearly? Blood altered magic. It amplified certain qualities, particularly intent. It meant her stitches would not simply protect or strengthen. They would respond to something deeper. Emotion. Will. Identity. She set the paper down, steadying her hands.

A soft knock came at the door. Mira lifted her head. A young attendant peeked inside.

"The princess is ready for you."

Mira stood on legs that felt too light. She collected the folder and followed the attendant through a tall archway, into a corridor lined with banners in muted gold. Sunlight streamed through glass windows high above the walkway, giving the palace a glow that belonged more to morning frost than warmth.

Two guards stood before a set of open doors. They watched her approach but said nothing. The attendant stepped aside. Mira walked forward, breathing evenly as she entered the room.

Princess Selene sat alone at a long table of pale carved wood. She wore no crown, only a simple circlet of polished steel above neatly braided blond hair. Her posture was straight, not rigid, her expression composed and unreadable. She gave no acknowledgment of Mira's presence until the seamstress came close and bowed.

"Rise," Selene said.

She did not speak loudly. Her voice carried through the room without effort. Mira raised her head slowly. Selene's eyes were clear gray, pale enough to reflect the light. She gestured for Mira to sit in the chair opposite her.

"You are Mira Nerielle," the princess stated, not asked.

"Yes, Your Highness."

"I requested a discreet artisan. They sent you. That means you understand the importance of restraint. I expect you to keep your work within the bounds assigned."

Mira nodded.

Selene folded her hands lightly on the table. "You are here because you can follow instructions. I do not need creativity. I need precision. Do not stitch anything that has not been specified. Do not revise the structure for aesthetic reasons. Function outweighs appearance in this matter."

Her tone remained calm throughout. Not harsh. Not cruel. Mira felt the weight of each word like stone being placed in a line.

"Yes, Your Highness."

"Good. Then we will discuss the enchantments."

Mira straightened slightly.

"As you know," Selene continued, "we are performing a binding rite. This marriage is a tool of stability. Commander Kael's loyalty is unchallenged, but loyalty alone cannot guarantee peace among our allies. The rite will grant both sides assurance of unity. It requires expertise and discretion from all participants."

She tilted her head slightly toward the papers Mira held. "You have reviewed the binding requirements."

"Yes," Mira said softly.

"Then you know that spellcasters will not be involved. The garment must carry the magic. That is deliberate."

Mira kept her voice steady. "I understand."

"Do you know why?" Selene asked.

The question gave Mira pause. She tried to answer without stepping beyond her role. "If there are no spellcasters, then no mage can influence or manipulate the rite. The garment will hold the magic without personal bias."

Selene nodded once in approval. "Exactly. A garment cannot betray. A person can. That is why you must be exact."

Her calmness made the air feel tight. Mira shifted slightly in her chair, careful not to fidget.

"You will place protective enchantments in the outer layer," Selene continued. "They must shield against hostile magic. Foreign mages should not be able to tamper with the ceremony. You will also place a binding enchantment beneath the armor lining. It will solidify the oath. It will not restrict his will. It will only confirm the union."

Mira tried to hide her reaction. She understood that wording. The binding enchantment would confirm loyalty through marriage, symbolically and magically. It would not force obedience. It would reinforce it.

"Do not confuse reinforcement with coercion," Selene said, as though reading Mira's thoughts. "This is not enslavement. It is assurance. A marriage must be honored by both sides. Without stability, no kingdom survives."

Her words were matter of fact, spoken without physical or emotional pressure. She could have been discussing grain imports rather than the manipulation of a person's life.

Mira collected her thoughts. She stayed quiet, waiting for the princess to continue.

"There is one aspect of the rite you must prepare for with utmost care," Selene said. "You may ask questions only relating to technical matters. Nothing beyond that. Do you understand?"

"Yes, Your Highness."

"Good." Selene tapped the table lightly with one finger. "You saw the note regarding the wearer's blood."

Mira's chest tightened slightly. "Yes."

"You may be wondering how much contact is necessary. The amount is small. A prick. A ritual cut. Nothing life threatening."

She paused, watching Mira closely. "Are you comfortable stitching a garment intended to respond to blood magic?"

Mira swallowed carefully. She forced her voice to remain calm. "I am able to do so if given instruction and the proper materials."

"You will receive both," Selene said. "Do not worry about the ceremony itself. You will not witness it. Your work ends once the garment is placed on him."

Mira nodded, though she had a question she could not keep down. She tried to phrase it without stepping into forbidden territory.

"How should the garment respond to the blood? Will it anchor protection to the wearer, or will it channel through the binding enchantment?"

Selene considered her for a long moment. Mira feared she had gone too far, but the princess finally spoke.

"It will do both. The protection shields him. The binding solidifies the oath. One without the other is inadequate. You must balance both functions so one does not overpower the other. That is why you were chosen. They believe you will not try to innovate. Only follow."

Mira felt the implication clearly. They did not want a powerful caster. They wanted someone who would not impose her will through craft. She nodded again, careful not to reveal anything through her expression.

Selene took a slow breath, then spoke more broadly. "Commander Kael is a symbol of the crown's strength. Ritual garments must respect that strength without absorbing it or directing it. Treat his power as a force to be acknowledged, not controlled."

Mira's pulse beat faster at those words. She remembered the man she had saved. Not a symbol. A man in pain. A man trying to live.

Selene continued. "There are rumors about the Commander. You may have heard some. Do not concern yourself with his past. It has no value here. You are not responsible for who he is. Only for what he wears."

Her tone remained neutral. Mira could not decide whether that neutrality made her more comfortable or more uneasy.

"If you fail," Selene said, "your mistake will not hurt me. It will not hurt him. It will hurt the kingdom. And the kingdom will protect itself first."

The room felt colder, though she had not raised her voice. She did not threaten Mira. She did not need to. Her logic was the threat.

Mira bowed her head slightly. "I will not fail, Your Highness."

Selene stood. Mira rose immediately.

"We will review drafts tomorrow. You may return to your work."

Two guards stepped forward as if they had been waiting for a cue. Selene left the room with the quiet confidence of someone who never needed to fear consequences. Mira remained standing until the door closed behind the princess.

When she finally stepped away from the table, her legs felt stiff.

She walked out past the guards, down the hall, and back toward her workroom. She did not see Iris until she was nearly at the door. The steward studied her face carefully.

"You did not speak out of turn," Iris said quietly. "Good."

Mira opened the workroom door and stepped inside. She closed it and leaned her back against the wood, letting herself breathe fully. Only then did her emotions catch up.

The garment she would make was not just clothing. It was an agreement. A safeguard. A tether. Ritual magic would pass through her hands and into the life of a man the palace both relied on and feared. The princess had not shown hatred or warmth, only logic. That made her more dangerous than any rumor.

Mira looked at the fabric waiting on her table. The morning sunlight touched the silk as though it were something sacred.

She stepped forward and began preparing her needle.

The stakes were no longer just aesthetics. They were blood and loyalty. And she would be the one to stitch them together.

4

The first stitch of the day was always the most important. It set the rhythm, the feel, the way her hands would move for hours after. Mira liked that moment, that quiet second where nothing had been started yet and everything was still possible.

Today, she dreaded it.

She stood at her worktable and looked down at the pale silk spread in front of her. The fabric glowed softly in the morning light that filtered through the high window. Tools were neatly arranged: shears, pins, chalk, needles in their small wooden case, thread in careful rows. Everything was in order. Everything was ready.

Her hands refused to move.

The conversation with Princess Selene replayed in her mind. Protection and binding. Blood and certainty. Assurance, not coercion. That was what Selene had said. The words were polite and clean, as if they were talking about the reinforcement of a wall rather than the shaping of a life.

Mira rubbed her thumb over her fingertip, feeling the faint roughness where needles had hardened the skin. She could not afford to sit frozen. There would be a fitting soon. For that, she needed at least partial stitching completed, even if it was just enough to give shape to the garments. She knew the measurements from the palace records, but she had never trusted numbers on a page more than her own eye.

She picked up a needle.

The familiar weight settled into her fingers. The magic in her palm stirred, recognizing the start of work. It rose from its resting place beneath her skin, like a warm tide. She took a slow breath and limited the rise. Not too much, not yet.

Mira threaded the needle with fine white silk and anchored the first stitch near the shoulder of the garment's outer layer. Her motions were steady. She focused only on the path of the needle, the way it pierced and returned, the particular give of enchanted silk. Her magic slipped with it, sinking into each loop and tug. It fastened to the cloth the way roots fastened under soil.

She let the enchantment settle in a shallow way at first. A thin reinforcement, nowhere near the strength it would eventually hold. There was time to deepen it later. For now, she needed a foundation.

Her thoughts wandered anyway.

Commander Kael Ardyn.

She pictured him as she had last seen him before this commission was even a thought, collapsed in a field tent that smelled of blood and smoke. His skin had been gray with shock, a smear of red across his shoulder and chest where a blade had torn through armor. He had been surrounded by healers who whispered to one another with panic just beneath their professionalism.

He had been dying.

She remembered slipping into the tent, pretending to belong, carrying water and bandages. No one had stopped her. No one had noticed her at all. She had knelt beside his pallet and pulled the blanket up under his chin while a healer shouted for more salve near the entrance.

She had touched his skin. She had felt the sluggish beat of his pulse.

Her magic had moved on instinct. It had poured into him, not through cloth, not through a needle, but through her hand. She had not known if it would help. It had simply rushed out with such force that she thought it might tear her apart.

His breath had steadied. Color had crept back into his face. A slow, rough sound escaped his throat, almost a word. She had pulled away before he fully returned to consciousness. She had left the tent and disappeared into the crowded camp, shaking so hard she had barely been able to hold on to her satchel.

The needle in her hand pricked her finger.

Mira hissed softly and jerked back. A bright dot of red swelled on the pad of her finger, startling against her pale skin. She watched, fascinated and uneasy, as the drop grew and then slid sideways, landing on the edge of the silk.

Her heart clenched.

Her blood soaked into the cloth, a tiny spot that spread in a faint pink bloom. The fabric reacted. A warm shiver passed through it as if it were breathing. The magic within her responded, reaching instinctively toward that contact. She snatched her hand back and pressed the cut against her apron to stop the bleeding.

"Fool," she whispered to herself.

It was only a small touch. The ritual called for his blood, not hers. Still, magic tied to blood behaved differently than magic tied only to thread. It remembered things. It held impressions. Her blood carried memories of the night she had saved him. It carried the knowledge of what she feared and what she could not admit.

Mira reached for a damp cloth and quickly blotted the stain. The silk lightened. The mark faded, though she doubted it was truly gone. Some trace would remain, tucked inside the threads. She would have to cut that section away or layer over it. She could not risk leaving her blood in a place meant for him.

Once the finger stopped bleeding, she wrapped it with a thin strip of linen from her supply drawer. It was clumsy, but it would do. She set the used cloth aside carefully. She would burn it later.

She stared at the garment again. Her magic was still unsettled. It pressed against the edges of her control, wanting to move, wanting to bind.

"This is only fabric," she told herself quietly. "Not him."

She forced her hands back to work. If she sat still, her thoughts would drown her. Movement was safer.

She stitched steadily, letting the magic slide into the seams with every pass. It felt differently now, a little sharper, a little more focused, as if the accidental touch of blood had woken something in it. She refused to think about that. She concentrated on alignment, on keeping the pattern precise. Outer layer, collar, sleeves. The work pulled her forward.

Time blurred. Morning thickened toward midday. She only stopped when a knock sounded on the door.

"Enter," Mira called softly.

Iris Merrow opened the door and stepped inside. She looked at the fabric, at the measured pieces and careful progress. She nodded once in approval. "You have begun weaving the enchantments."

"Yes," Mira said. "Only the first pass. There is much more to do."

"You will increase the strength once fitting is confirmed," Iris said. It was not a question.

"Yes."

Iris crossed to the table, her eyes keen. "The Commander will attend his first fitting this afternoon. You should have something for him to wear, even if it is not the final piece."

Mira's grip on her needle tightened. "This afternoon."

"Yes." Iris looked at her, as if measuring her reaction. "Is that a problem, Seamstress?"

"No," Mira answered quickly. "Only sooner than I expected."

"Royal schedules change when they wish," Iris said. "Learn to adapt. You will fit him in this room. I will be present. The Commander will be accompanied by guards. You will maintain formal respect at all times."

Mira nodded. Her mind raced through what needed to be ready. "The outer layer will not be finished. I can have a partial shell for line and movement. The underlayer can be pinned. I will have measuring ribbons ready."

"Do what you must," Iris said. "He will not give you much time. He does not enjoy standing still."

With that, Iris left.

Mira sat for a moment after the door closed, feeling as if the floor beneath her had tilted. She had thought she would have more time before she had to stand in front of him. No such luck.

She set aside the near completed section of the outer layer and reached for a simpler garment form. For a first fitting, she did not need full ceremonial structure. She needed shape, range of motion, the way the cloth lay against his shoulders. This part could be mostly plain.

She cut a neutral vest from spare fabric, one that would mimic the weight of the final silk without carrying the same enchantments. She sewed quickly, fingers flying with practiced speed that surprised even her. She set the vest aside and prepared a belt, sleeves that could be pinned and a collar form. Each piece would help her measure how the final garment should move with him.

Her magic tried to seep even into these simple pieces. She held it back firmly. There was no need for extra reaction when he was present. She needed her stitching to behave like any ordinary tailor's work. If he noticed something strange, he might ask questions. She had no desire to lie to the Commander's face.

When she had prepared as much as she could, she cleaned the table surface and brushed stray threads away. She checked her apron, straightened her hair and washed her hands thoroughly, rubbing away any trace of nervous sweat.

There was still time before afternoon. She returned to her seat and stitched quietly, using the hours to deepen the enchantment along the inner seams where protection would rest. With each stitch, she thought of shielding, not binding. Of repelling harm, not tethering a life. She reinforced the idea in her mind so strongly that her magic began to follow the thought almost on its own.

By the time the sun had shifted and the light through the window turned warm instead of pale, she heard it.

Footsteps in the corridor. Heavier than a servant's. More than one pair.

Her needle paused mid stitch. Her breath stilled. The knock on the door came a moment later.

Iris opened the door without waiting for Mira's answer. She stepped inside first, smoothing her skirts with one hand. Behind her, two palace guards entered, then moved aside.

He came in last.

Commander Kael Ardyn filled the doorway. He was taller than she remembered, or perhaps memory had been too hazy to be precise. Broad shoulders, straight posture, dark hair cut short enough to stay out of his eyes. A faint scar crossed the bridge of his nose and another traced his jaw, pale against tanned skin. His eyes were a cool, steady brown that took in the room in one sweep.

He wore a simple uniform, dark and clean, with no ceremonial ornaments. Only a thin silver stripe at the collar marked his rank. His presence did not blaze or thunder. It settled, heavy and quiet, like a stone dropping into deep water.

All the rumors about him killing without restraint did not show in his face. His expression was calm, almost bored, but there was something underneath, a restrained energy, the sense of someone who could move very fast if he chose to.

Mira forced herself to bow. Her ribs felt tight.

"Commander," Iris said with a respectful inclination of her head. "This is Seamstress Mira Nerielle. She has been assigned to your ceremonial attire."

Kael's gaze shifted to her. For a moment, there was only polite recognition. Then his brows drew in slightly, as if he were trying to focus on something just out of sight.

"We have met," he said.

Mira's heart gave a painful jolt. "No, Commander. I do not believe so."

His eyes narrowed a fraction, not in suspicion, but in thought. "At least, it seems that way."

His voice was lower than she remembered from the battlefield, but of course it would be. He had not been in control then. Now he spoke with the steady cadence of someone used to being obeyed.

"You may approach, Seamstress," Iris prompted in a low voice.

Mira moved forward, hands steady only because she did not allow them any other option. She stopped at the table where the plain vest lay.

"We will begin with basic measurements and fit, Commander," she said quietly. "This piece will help me adjust the lines before cutting into more valuable cloth. With your permission."

He studied her for another moment. "Proceed."

She held the vest up. "Would you remove your outer coat, please?"

He unbuttoned the dark coat without protest and laid it across the back of a chair. The tunic underneath clung lightly to his frame. Mira glimpsed the shift of muscle at his shoulders. There was a thickened line at his left shoulder where a scar must rest under the fabric, the same area she remembered bleeding on the battlefield. Her throat tightened.

He slipped into the vest. She stepped around him, careful to keep a professional distance while still doing her work. She fastened the buttons down his chest and adjusted the shoulders, pulling the fabric lightly to test its hang.

She felt the warmth of him, even without touching skin. It seeped through the cloth, through the air between them. She tried to ignore it. She focused on the way the seams sat.

"Lift your arms horizontally, please," she said.

He complied. The motion stretched the fabric across his shoulders. She checked the range.

"Any tightness?" she asked.

"No," he said. His voice was close, just next to her ear. She tried not to react.

She circled him, adjusting small pins, marking with chalk where she would need more room. His posture remained steady. He did not fidget, did not complain. He was the opposite of most noble clients, who sighed and groaned at every pin prick and demanded comfort above all. He stood like this was just another duty, no more or less interesting than practicing formations or meeting with generals.

"How often will I be needed for these fittings?" he asked casually.

"Several times before the ceremony," Mira replied. "If possible, Commander. Some adjustments will be necessary as the enchantments deepen. The cloth can change texture when magic settles fully."

"Does that make it uncomfortable to wear?" he asked.

"Not if I do my work correctly," she said.

She heard a faint huff of breath that might have been amusement.

"You have stitched for other rituals?" he asked.

For a moment, she almost answered with the truth, that she had only worked small spells into garments, protective lines for minor nobles, nothing on this scale. She caught herself and chose a safer version.

"I have reinforced garments that carried minor rites," she said. "This is my first binding of this type."

"And they trusted you with it," he said. It was not quite a question. More an observation.

"They trust my silence," she found herself saying before she could stop.

She almost winced. That was too honest. Kael turned his head slightly, as if weighing her words.

"Silence can be as valuable as skill," he said at last. "Sometimes more."

He did not say it kindly or unkindly. It was just fact.

She moved on quickly. "I will need to measure your arms more precisely. If you would extend your right arm."

He held it out. She took her measuring ribbon and wrapped it lightly around his bicep, elbow, wrist. Her fingers brushed against the fabric of his sleeve, and through it, the heat of his skin.

Her magic surged. It slid down the measuring ribbon, hungry for contact. She clenched her jaw and forced it back, trying to imagine a wall in her mind, something solid and immovable. The magic recoiled, but not completely. It left a faint warmth in the ribbon, a subtle vibration.

Kael's gaze flicked down to the ribbon.

"Is it supposed to feel like that?" he asked.

Her stomach dropped. Of course he would notice. He was a soldier. His body knew when something foreign touched it.

Mira looked up at him, then quickly away. "The fabric holds a residual charge from the enchanted cloth, Commander. It is harmless. If it is uncomfortable, I can replace it."

He turned his hand, flexing his fingers. "It is not painful. Only different."

"Then it is acceptable?" she asked.

"For now."

She finished measuring his right arm and moved to the left. The scar at his shoulder pulled the fabric slightly. She noted the adjustment she would need to make.

As she worked, the room seemed to shrink. Iris stood near the window, watching with keen interest. The guards waited close to the door, their expressions deliberately blank. The air felt thick, full of the quiet sound of her own breathing and the faint rustle of fabric when Kael shifted.

She moved in front of him to measure his chest next. She avoided meeting his gaze, but she could feel it on her, steady and curious.

"You are nervous," he said softly.

The words stopped her for a second. She looked up before she could stop herself.

His eyes were not hard. They were assessing, yes, but not cruel. He looked at her the way he might look at a weather pattern. Trying to understand if it meant rain.

"Yes, Commander," she said. There was no point lying. "This is a significant commission."

"Significant for whom?" he asked. "For you, or for them?"

"Both," she said.

He considered that. "You work alone in here?"

"Steward Merrow supervises," Mira said. "Supplies are delivered as needed."

"And no one else touches the cloth," he said.

"Yes."

He exhaled slowly. "Good."

She hesitated. "You prefer that?"

"I prefer to know who has had their hands on something that will sit near my skin during a ceremony I do not control," he said. His tone remained even, but there was something underneath it. Wariness. Refusal to be blind.

"You do not trust the ritual," she said before she could stop the words. They slipped out, unplanned.

His gaze sharpened. Iris shifted near the window, but did not intervene. Mira swallowed and focused on the measuring ribbon, wrapping it around his chest at the level just under his arms.

"I trust the crown to do what it believes is necessary," he said. "That is not the same as trusting every process they prefer."

Mira did not answer. She finished the measurement and stepped back.

He watched her for another moment, then a faint line appeared between his brows.

"I know your face," he said quietly.

Her heart slammed against her ribs.

"No, Commander," she said. "I am only a seamstress."

He studied her, eyes searching. "I have seen many faces. Most I forget. A few remain for reasons I cannot always explain."

Iris spoke then, sharp enough to cut the moment without raising her voice. "Commander, if we may proceed, the seamstress has limited time to record your measurements."

Kael glanced at her, then back to Mira. The intensity in his gaze faded, replaced by cool practicality.

"Of course," he said. "What next, Seamstress?"

She swallowed and gestured to the chair. "If you would sit, I must check how the cloth falls while you are at rest. The ceremony will involve standing and kneeling, perhaps. I need to ensure the garment does not restrict movement."

He sat. The plain vest pulled slightly at the shoulders. She adjusted it, pinning here and there, making notes on her parchment. He moved his arms when she asked, turned his head, leaned forward. Her mind took in every small detail, storing it away for later. It was almost a relief to sink into the technical aspects. Cloth did not look back at her. Cloth did not ask questions.

When she finished, she stepped away. "That will be enough for the first fitting, Commander. I will need you again once I set the primary seams."

"Very well," he said, rising. He unbuttoned the vest and removed it, handing it back to her without ceremony. For a brief second, his fingers brushed her wrist.

Her magic reacted again. Not in a surge this time, but in a quick, bright pulse, as if acknowledging something strongly familiar. A pattern it remembered.

Kael paused. His brow furrowed slightly, but he said nothing. He put his coat back on and fastened it. The guards straightened.

Before he left, his gaze returned to the table, to the partially stitched outer garment resting there. His hand reached out, almost absently, and his knuckles grazed the edge of the silk.

The reaction was instant.

The cloth warmed under his touch, far stronger than it had for her. The threads she had enchanted along the inner seam flared, not visibly, but she felt it. The air around the garment prickled. It was like the sensation of a storm gathering, just at the edge of awareness.

Mira's breath caught. She stepped forward quickly, as if to adjust the fabric. In truth, she was trying to shield the reaction from Iris's view.

Kael drew his hand back, eyes narrowing faintly. "That one is different."

Mira forced her voice steady. "It has received more attention than the others. You felt a greater charge, that is all."

His gaze lingered on the cloth. For a moment, she wondered if he would press the issue. Then he nodded slowly.

"Keep your attention on it, then," he said. "If I must wear something strange, I prefer it to be effective."

Iris gave a brief, tight smile. "The seamstress understands the importance of her work, Commander."

He gave a faint incline of his head to both of them, then turned and left the room, guards falling into step behind him. The door closed softly.

The silence that followed felt deep and strange.

Iris did not speak immediately. She walked to the table and studied the garment. Her eyes narrowed.

"You have laid a strong foundation already," she said. "Perhaps stronger than necessary for this stage."

Mira kept her face neutral. "I wanted to ensure the base was stable before proceeding."

"Do not get ahead of the specifications," Iris said. "Princess Selene expects balance. Too much focus on one type of enchantment can cause unpredictable reactions later."

"I know," Mira said quietly.

"Do you?" Iris's gaze sharpened. "If you overbind protection to him, it may cost protection for the rite itself. Remember, this is not a personal shield. It is a political garment."

Mira nodded once. Iris lingered a moment longer, then turned toward the door.

"You will be informed of the next fitting time," the steward said. "Do not waste the hours you have."

When she was alone again, Mira finally let her shoulders sag. Her hands shook slightly. She set the plain vest aside and moved to the outer garment. She pressed her fingers lightly against the seam he had touched.

The cloth was still warm. Not just from his hand. The warmth pulsed beneath the surface, a gentle beat that matched something inside her. Her magic flowed toward it almost eagerly, as if drawn to a kindred presence.

"You are not supposed to do that," she murmured to the garment, as if it could hear. "You are meant to protect the bride. Not him."

The fabric did not answer, of course. It simply held the enchantment she had placed in it, strengthened unexpectedly by his touch. Or by her reaction to it. She was not sure which played the greater part.

Mira sat and laid the garment flat. She closed her eyes and rested her palm over the seam. She reached into the enchantment, gently, the way she might test water for heat. She did not push, only listened.

What she sensed unsettled her.

The magic had anchored itself around an impression. Not a clear picture or a name, but a sense of solidity, of a specific weight and presence. It had recognized him. It had begun to attune not simply to a wearer, but to that wearer.

If she continued stitching without correction, the protection would likely favor him regardless of who stood at his side. It would still shield the area around him, but any blood bond might lean toward his survival over the rite's symbolism.

She bit her lower lip, thinking quickly.

This was what Selene had warned her against without using those words. The garment must not choose. It must serve the purpose assigned. Any slant toward something personal could unbalance the magic. Her heart had created a tilt without her permission. Her memories and fear and reluctant care had seeped into the stitches.

Mira pulled her hand back and stared at the cloth.

"I cannot let you decide," she said softly.

She considered unpicking the seams she had laid. Removing them now, before the enchantment settled deep, might be possible. It would cost her hours of work. It would also mean discarding the silk touched by her blood earlier. That might be for the best. But part of her hesitated.

When she reached into the enchantment, she had felt something else beneath the dangerous tilt. She had felt a desire to shield, pure and strong. A wish to keep harm from reaching him. It was her magic, but it was also something his presence had called out of it.

If she removed it, the garment would be safer. It would also be more empty. More obedient.

She drew a slow breath and took up her seam ripper.

For now, she told herself, logic must win. Princess Selene was not wrong about one thing. The garment served the kingdom first. If she allowed it to serve her heart instead, the consequences would fall on her, and possibly on him, if the rite went wrong.

One careful stitch at a time, she began to pull out the thread she had laid that morning.

As she worked, a thought settled like dust in the back of her mind.

No matter how many threads she removed, no matter how many she replaced, the first connection had been made. Her magic had recognized him. The cloth had felt him. That echo might fade, but it would never fully erase.

Binding was not just an action. It was a choice. Even if she denied it, some part of her had already made one.

She cut the last of the thread and laid the garment down. The silk lay quiet again, but not empty. The faint sense of him remained, like a ghost in the fabric.

Mira pressed her hands to the table and lowered her head. Her eyes burned, but she did not cry. She would not waste tears on what she could not change.

"The garment will be for the rite," she whispered to the silent room. "It will do as it is meant to. It will not give itself to you."

Her magic stirred under her skin, as if in disagreement.

She straightened and reached for a fresh needle. The afternoon light slid across the floor, stretching toward evening. She threaded the needle with new silk.

With every new stitch, she tried to think of neutrality. Of balance. Of duty. Yet every time she closed her eyes, she saw him standing in her workroom, quiet and self contained, eyes sharp as if trying to remember where he had seen her.

Every time her magic slid into the cloth, it remembered his touch.

By the time the sun began to set, the garment had taken on new structure. The seams were cleaner, more controlled. The enchantment was more even. She had done her work well. Anyone else examining it would see nothing but skill.

She, however, felt the quiet truth beneath it.

No matter how carefully she stitched, the thread of him ran through it now, faint and stubborn.

The garment intended to protect a marriage had already chosen its first loyalty.

And Mira did not know how to unchoose him without tearing herself apart in the process.

5

Rain softened the palace walls that morning. It fell lightly, just a thin curtain of gray water that trickled through the gutters and made the cobblestones shine like dark glass. Mira listened to the sound of it from her workroom. The tapping on the high window reminded her of needles against cloth, constant and quiet and easy to ignore, unless one paid attention.

She worked through it.

The garment lay across her table, partially fitted after the earlier adjustments. Sleeves now rested in place but required refinement. The collar shape returned to a neutral state after she had undone the earlier seams. Every movement of the needle demanded discipline. Every stitch asked her to remember neutrality, balance, purpose. The garment must hold protection for a marriage she had no right to judge.

She worked slowly. She needed to keep her magic steady. She repeated the same thought under her breath like a calming spell: Protect the rite, not the man. Protect the rite, not the man.

Her magic disagreed. It stirred whenever she remembered how he had looked at her during the fitting. Calm, controlled, not warm but not dismissive. Someone who did not treat her like furniture. That was dangerous in its own way.

She set her needle down and flexed her fingers. A dull ache throbbed at the joints from working too tightly. She rubbed her palm against her apron and tried to relax. The rain soothed nothing.

A knock sounded on the door. Mira looked up.

"Enter," she called.

The door opened to reveal Iris Merrow. The steward stepped inside with her usual controlled posture. Her hair was pinned so neatly that not a single strand moved. She held a small ledger in her hand.

"Commander Kael will return for fitting shortly," Iris said.

Mira's breath caught in quiet surprise. She had expected at least another day, perhaps two. "Is there a change in schedule?"

"Yes," Iris replied. "The Commander requested an earlier fitting. I assume he wishes to settle matters more quickly."

That seemed unlikely. Men such as Kael did not rush for the sake of clothing. Something else must have changed.

"When will he arrive?" Mira asked.

Iris glanced toward the window as though she could see through the rain. "He is already on the floor. Prepare yourself."

She left without waiting for Mira to speak.

Mira exhaled slowly, then stood. Her heart shifted into a faster rhythm, not chaotic but steady in a way that warned her how important this moment might be. She straightened the cloth on the table, brushed away loose threads and set out the measuring ribbons again, even though she might not need them. She adjusted her apron and checked her hands for stray chalk dust.

The knock came again, less patient this time. Mira composed herself.

"Enter," she said.

The door opened. Kael stepped through.

He was not dressed in formal uniform this time. His tunic was dark but plain, without markings except a small emblem on the collar. The fabric clung slightly with moisture from the rain outside. His hair, normally kept neatly back, fell a little looser across his forehead, dampened by the weather. His expression was calm, but the way he stood said otherwise. There was tension in his jaw, an unusual tautness across his shoulders.

He looked tired.

Mira bowed her head lightly. "Commander."

He nodded, acknowledging her greeting without ceremony. "Seamstress."

A brief pause followed. He did not move closer on his own. He stood still as if considering something. Mira waited. Silence had become familiar between them. Silence felt safer than conversation. She approached him slowly.

"If you would remove your outer layer again," she said, gesturing gently toward the coat. "We will continue fitting the collar and sleeves."

He unbuttoned the coat without speaking, then draped it over the chair exactly as he had before. The motion seemed slower today. Heavy. She wondered how little sleep he had gotten.

He stepped toward her, closer than necessary at first, then seemed to catch himself and adjusted his distance by a small step back. She did not comment. She lifted the partial garment carefully and held it toward him.

"May I?" she asked.

He inclined his head.

She helped him slip into the garment. Her fingers brushed briefly against the inside of the collar as she adjusted it. She tried to ignore the warmth at her fingertips. Her magic stretched toward him without her permission. She reined it back sharply.

"Lift your arms again, please."

He obeyed, but slower this time. As he raised them, Mira noticed the faint tightness in his movements. Not from the garment. From his body. The muscles at his shoulders pulled more stiffly than they had before. His breath caught slightly when he lifted all the way up. He hid it almost immediately, but she caught the ghost of the effort.

"You have strain at the shoulder," she said quietly. She could not help the observation. It slipped out as naturally as breathing.

Kael lowered his arms. "It will pass."

"Has there been fighting?" she asked before thinking better.

"No." His answer came too quickly and then softened. "There was no war. Only decisions."

The way he spoke the word decisions made it sound heavier than battle.

Her fingers paused over the sleeve seam she was adjusting. "Decisions can be difficult to carry."

He glanced at her. His eyes did not harden or soften. They studied her quietly. "Some of them should not be made," he said.

"That is not always your choice," she replied.

His jaw tightened slightly. "It should be."

He fell silent. She continued adjusting the sleeve, pretending she had not just heard a dangerous truth slide out of him. She chalked the line and tied the fabric lightly.

She stepped in front of him to examine the collar next. Her fingers brushed the edge of the cloth where it rested near his throat. He held still. Too still. Most clients flinched at such proximity. He remained steady but rigid, like someone bracing for something else entirely.

She looked up, just slightly, and met his eyes before she even realized she had done it. He was watching her. Not intensely. Simply watching, as if he were trying to understand a pattern.

His voice came out barely above conversational tone. "You asked if there was fighting."

Mira did not answer. She waited. She did not dare encourage him, yet something in her stayed open.

"There was no battlefield," he said. "Only nobles at a table. They argue like men with swords but refuse to bleed. They want war without any cost to themselves."

He paused.

"I cannot give them what they want," he continued. "But I cannot refuse what the crown asks."

She swallowed quietly. "The crown expects you to marry the princess."

"Yes."

"And you accepted."

His mouth tightened a little. "I accepted because they said it would protect the border. Because they framed it as peace. Not because I want it."

Mira's hand stilled on the collar. She did not remove it. She did not speak. The room seemed to hold its breath along with her.

Kael continued, voice flat with exhaustion. "A marriage for strategy is not new. I do not object to duty. I object to being told it will bring peace when the same men who arrange it dream of war."

Her heart pressed hard against her ribs. She felt the urge to say something that would be a mistake. Still, the words formed.

"Do you trust the crown?"

He studied her again. "I trust the kingdom needs stability. Trusting the crown is something different."

She lowered her hands slowly, letting the collar fall naturally into place. "And you are part of that stability."

"I am what they use for it," he corrected.

Her next question came softly. "Does that frighten you?"

She had not meant to ask that. The moment the words left her mouth, she regretted them. She looked down quickly, as if focusing on a seam would make the question disappear.

Kael did not answer immediately. When he finally spoke, his voice was quieter.

"I am not afraid of duty. I am afraid of becoming something that has no place beyond it."

Mira's throat tightened. She understood too well the fear of being only one thing, valued only for what one could do, not who one was. She almost said something. Almost told him she had once saved him without knowing his name. Almost revealed that she had seen a version of him no one else had seen. A man dying, not a weapon.

Instead, she whispered, "No one chooses to be used."

His gaze lowered slightly. "Perhaps. But some of us do not get to refuse it."

He did not sound angry. He sounded tired. Bone deep tired.

Her hands moved almost without thought. She reached toward the collar, as if to adjust a seam, but her fingers brushed against his neck. For a heartbeat, her skin met his.

Her magic surged.

Not wildly. Not breaking. But intensely. It poured into the cloth like warm breath, thickening the threads just enough to reinforce them. The garment tightened around his shoulders. Not constricting, not harmful, but protective. The seams flexed with a subtle force, as if shielding him.

Kael inhaled slightly. He noticed. His eyes flicked to hers.

"Something changed," he said.

Mira pulled her hand back too quickly. "The enchantment settled. It will stabilize after more stitching."

He watched her for a moment longer, quiet and perceptive. She kept her focus on the collar edge, pretending she had not felt her own magic respond as if it had a will of its own.

She needed something to distract him. Her mind scrambled for a safe topic. "The collar will fit more comfortably once I adjust the inner lining. There is a slight shift caused by your posture today. If you would relax your shoulders, it would show how the garment settles under less tension."

His brows lowered. "Relax?"

"Yes," she said. "Lower your shoulders. Breathe normally. Do not stand at attention."

He hesitated, then allowed his posture to loosen. Not fully, but enough. The garment shifted with him. The seams eased around his chest. The collar adjusted. The magic responded again, less aggressively this time, more like a quiet sigh.

She noted the movement. "Better."

He gave a faint sound that might have been a dry laugh. "You give orders like a surgeon."

Mira blinked. "I apologize."

"No," he said. "It was not a complaint."

She felt a strange warmth at that. She shut it down immediately. Whatever familiarity she thought she felt was dangerous. He could not know her. She could not know him. They were not friends. They were two people performing separate duties in the same room.

She focused on pinning the sleeve edge. He watched her hands move, but did not speak. Silence returned, not heavy this time, just present. When she finished, she stepped back.

"That is all for this stage, Commander," she said.

He nodded. "When will you need me again?"

"After I reinforce the inner seams," she said. "Two days. Perhaps three."

"Send word," he replied. "I will come."

He reached for his coat. She expected him to leave without another word. Instead, he paused at the table, looking down at the garment's pieces.

"You asked about fighting," he said quietly, without turning his head toward her. "There are wars fought without swords. They leave scars no healer can mend."

She looked at him, unsure if he wanted a response.

His next words came just as quietly. "If I am to marry, I would prefer it not be to secure someone else's ambition."

She almost said, It should not cost you yourself. The sentence hovered in her throat like a stitch waiting to be placed.

Her voice came out differently. "It should not cost anyone."

He regarded her for a moment. Then he nodded and left without ceremony. The guards followed. The door closed behind them.

Mira stood alone in the workroom. Rain still tapped against the window. The garment on the table seemed faintly alive under her gaze. The magic inside it pulsed with the memory of his presence. She could feel it through the threads, through her fingertips, through her bones.

Intimacy did not always need intention. Sometimes, it needed only truth. And truth, once shared, was difficult to unthread.

She sat at her table, laid the garment flat again, and breathed.

The cloth had tightened not because she willed it to, but because she had cared.

And that was more dangerous than any rumor whispered in palace halls.

6

The garment did not want to behave.

Mira could not have explained it any other way. She had worked enough enchanted cloth to know the feel of cooperative magic. This was not that. The seams listened, but only partly. The protection wanted to lean. Every time she thought she had finally coaxed the enchantment into a balanced path, it slid, subtle as a shadow, back toward the memory of him.

She pushed the needle through the cloth, guided the thread, and forced herself to think of the rite as a whole. Citizens watching, nobles gossiping quietly behind fans, the king's council holding their breath while the binding settled around a general and a princess in front of everyone. The garment was supposed to shield that moment. It could not belong to the general alone.

Still, her magic remembered his voice. It remembered the way he had said, I am afraid of becoming something that has no place beyond duty. It remembered his shoulders easing when she told him to relax, like a soldier who did not realize he had been standing at attention his whole life.

Her hand slipped. The stitch skewed, not visibly, but she felt it. A tiny pull toward one side, no more than a breath, as if the thread itself wanted to wrap around him.

Mira pulled the needle back out.

She unpicked the stitch slowly, teeth pressed together. Outside, rain still grazed the window in thin lines. The palace was quieter on such days. Footsteps softened on wet stone. Voices seemed less eager to rise. She wished her own thoughts would follow that example.

She had barely reset her needle when she heard the knock.

"Enter," she called.

The door opened. Iris Merrow stepped in, drier this time, with a folder tucked under one arm. She gave the room a swift, assessing glance. Her eyes lingered on the garment, tracing the line of its collar and sleeves, then returned to Mira.

"You have been busy," Iris said.

"Yes," Mira replied. "The protective seams are nearly complete. I will begin binding channels tomorrow."

"You will begin them today," Iris corrected. "Circumstances have changed."

Mira straightened. "Changed how?"

"Princess Selene will attend the next fitting," Iris said. "She means to observe the progress herself. She will arrive with the Commander."

Mira fumbled the needle. It slipped from her fingers and fell on the table with a soft ping. "Both of them. Together."

"Yes." Iris watched her reaction closely. "The princess wants to see how the garment moves. She also wants to witness how closely you follow her instructions. You will treat it as an ordinary fitting."

"Ordinary," Mira repeated, as if the word might reshape reality if she said it enough times.

"You will not let nerves interfere," Iris continued. "You will not let personal opinion about either of them appear on your face. You will ask no questions that do not directly concern the garment."

Mira picked up the needle and forced her fingers to stop shaking. "When will they arrive?"

"In a few hours," Iris said. "That gives you enough time to secure all tools, finish the current line of stitching and prepare the room.

Remove anything that suggests you have been experimenting beyond the specifications."

Mira felt the line as a rebuke. She glanced instinctively at the small bundle of scrap cloth in the corner where she had tested minor pattern variations. "Of course, Steward."

Iris followed her gaze. "Burn those before they come. You do not want the princess to suspect you have been weaving your own ideas into this project. Curiosity is expensive here."

"Yes," Mira said quietly. "I will handle it."

Iris started to leave, then paused at the door. "One more thing." Her voice lost some of its clipped sharpness. "The princess is not easily impressed. Do not try to impress her. Do your work honestly, and let it stand. Anything else will look like flattery."

Mira nodded. Iris gave a single approving look and left.

When the door closed, the room felt smaller.

Mira drew a breath and let it out slowly. This had always been a royal commission. She had always known the princess would want to see her own wedding garment. It should not have startled her. Yet something about Selene and Kael standing in the same space where she worked made her stomach twist.

She moved first to the scrap bundle. It contained bits of silk and thread where she had tested the strength of different stitch patterns. Some edges glowed faintly, still holding the residue of her magic. None of it was dangerous. All of it would look suspicious in the wrong eyes.

She took the bundle to the small hearth at the far wall, where a low fire burned to keep the chill from the room. She fed the scraps to the flames, one by one, until nothing remained but ash. Her magic flickered briefly with each piece consumed, as if saying goodbye.

Next, she organized the table. She removed extra tools, leaving only what she absolutely needed. Needles, thread, chalk, scissors. The main garment lay across the center surface, looking deceptively simple. Anyone else would see pale silk and careful lines. She saw choices, mistakes and an enchantment that refused to be as neutral as she wanted.

She ran her hand lightly over the cloth, not to add anything, just to soothe herself. The fabric warmed beneath her palm, answering like a living thing. She pulled her hand back before it could lean too strongly.

"You will behave," she murmured to it. "For both our sakes."

She spent the remaining time sewing quietly, setting small securing stitches at the back of the collar and along the lower hem. Each stitch was tiny, almost invisible. Each carried a whisper of magic, designed to distribute force evenly if the garment faced sudden impact. It was a kind of shield, subtle, always present. Given to the ritual, not just to a man.

When the palace bell tolled the hour, Mira cleaned her hands and straightened her clothing. She checked for stray threads, chalk marks, anything that might look unprofessional. The rain on the window had slowed to a mist. Light seeped through clouds, pale and diffused.

The knock came.

"Enter," Mira said, keeping her voice steady.

Iris opened the door first. She stepped in, posture even more precise than usual. Behind her, Princess Selene entered, followed by two guards. Mira bowed at once. She had expected Kael to come immediately after, but he was not there.

Selene wore a gown of deep blue, unadorned except for a slender chain at her throat. Her hair was braided back, pinned with small silver clips that caught the washed-out light. She moved with the same calm poise Mira remembered from their previous meeting. Her gaze went straight to the garment.

She did not smile. She did not frown. She simply studied it.

"Your Highness," Mira said quietly. "Welcome."

Selene approached the table. Iris stayed slightly behind her, close enough to assist if needed, far enough not to intrude.

"The work has progressed," Selene said. Her eyes followed the collar line, then the seams along the shoulders, then the sleeves. "Show me where you have placed the strongest protection so far."

Mira stepped closer and pointed. "The collar holds the primary warding. It stabilizes the flow. The shoulders and chest carry additional layers, mostly to deflect impact. I have not yet finalized the channels near the heart. That will wait until I can see how it rests on him when all pieces are attached."

Selene laid her fingertips lightly on the collar. Her skin barely touched the fabric.

Mira felt the garment tense.

The magic inside it did not react as it had to Kael. It did not warm in welcome or recognition. It stiffened. The seam under Selene's touch tightened subtly, as if bracing. Mira doubted anyone without sensitivity would notice. She noticed.

Selene's eyes narrowed by a fraction. "There is a strong response here, even unfinished."

"Some materials are more receptive than others," Mira replied. "The orchard silk carries enchantment easily."

"Do not insult me," Selene said in a flat tone. "I can feel there is more than simple receptiveness. This garment already recognizes something."

Mira fought the urge to press her palm over the seam, to block the line, to tell the magic to calm. "Your Highness, the enchantment is incomplete. It will settle differently once all elements are in place."

Selene glanced at her. "Perhaps."

Her gaze shifted back to the collar. Her expression remained calm, but Mira caught the faintest trace of something cooler in her eyes. Not anger. Assessment. As if she had just confirmed a suspicion.

"You have worked with attuned weaving before," Selene said. "I can feel the hint of it. The way the cloth is beginning to favor a particular resonance."

Mira swallowed. Attuned weaving. The phrase gave a too precise name to what she had hoped no one else would notice.

"I have some experience," Mira said carefully. "Only at minor levels. It helps garments adapt to the wearer's movements."

"It does more than that," Selene replied. "Attunement is a dangerous tool. Used unwisely, it shifts loyalty from purpose to person." Her gaze slid toward Mira with quiet weight. "Purposes change. People end."

Mira could not deny the truth in that. She did not trust her voice, so she stayed silent.

"Tell me something," Selene said. "When you began this work, did you think of the ritual first, or the man who would wear it?"

The question was light on the surface. The way she asked it made it sound like idle curiosity. It was not idle.

Mira focused on the table. "The ritual, Your Highness."

Selene watched her closely. "Are you certain?"

"Yes," Mira said. She forced herself to look up, even though every part of her wanted to stay bowed. "I understand the importance of the rite. I would not endanger it by making the garment personal."

Selene's eyes searched her face for a long moment. Mira tried to keep her expression smooth. She had learned how to be forgettable. She hoped that training held now.

Finally, Selene stepped back from the table. "Very well. We will see how it behaves when the Commander wears it."

As if summoned by the mention, footsteps approached in the corridor. The guards at the door straightened. A second later, the knock sounded again, more like a perfunctory tap than a request.

"Enter," Iris called this time.

Commander Kael stepped in with two of his own guards. Today, he wore his formal uniform. Dark coat, high collar, insignia at the chest. His hair was dry again, brushed back from his face in controlled lines. He looked more composed than he had during the last fitting, but the tiredness around his eyes remained.

He assessed the room quickly. His attention noted Selene, Iris, the guards. Then his gaze landed on Mira.

For a brief instant, his shoulders relaxed as if he had expected something worse. Perhaps more courtiers, more scrutinizers. Mira saw the small shift and felt something tighten inside her.

"Commander," Selene said, voice even. "Thank you for arriving promptly."

"Your Highness," he replied with a short bow. "You requested I present myself for the fitting. I am here."

Mira could not read his tone. It carried respect, but something else too. Distance maybe. Or carefulness.

Selene gestured toward the garment. "I want to see how the enchantments settle while you wear it. The seamstress informs me they are still forming."

"They are," Mira added quietly.

Kael gave a slight nod. "Then let us see what your efforts have done so far."

His gaze brushed over Mira again, one brief flicker that might have been reassurance, or simple acknowledgment. She was not sure which she wanted it to be.

Iris spoke up. "If you would remove your coat, Commander."

He did as requested. The room watched with more attention than such a simple act should warrant. He laid the coat over the chair and stepped closer to the table.

Mira lifted the garment. Her hands were steady. Her chest was not.

"Arms through, please," she said softly.

He slid his arms into the sleeves. The silk glided over his tunic, settling against his body with a familiarity that should not have been possible yet. She moved behind him to fasten the closures. Her fingers worked quickly, securing each small hook, smoothing each line.

She felt Selene's gaze on them both the entire time. It pressed like a weight across the back of her neck.

Once the garment was fully on, Mira stepped back to look. It fit closer now, more precise after her earlier adjustments. The shoulders aligned correctly. The collar framed his throat without choking. The length at the back brushed just above his knees.

"Lift your arms, please," she said. "Slowly."

He obeyed. The garment moved with him, stretching at the seams, then returning without strain. The enchantment shifted like a second skin, adapting to his posture.

Selene circled them, observing from different angles. "How does it feel?" she asked Kael.

He rotated his arms, testing the range. "It is light. Strong. I can feel the weave when I move."

"Does it restrict you?" Selene asked.

"No," he said. "If anything, it feels like it wants to anticipate me."

Mira's heart skipped. That was too close to the truth. Kael's instincts did not lie.

Selene's eyes flicked to Mira. "Is that intentional?"

"The cloth is designed to move with him," Mira said. "It prevents resistance at crucial points. That is what you instructed. Protection without hindrance."

"It also feels like someone is watching my back," Kael added in an almost absent tone. He rolled his shoulders, then relaxed. "Not unpleasant. Only unusual."

Selene's lips curved a fraction. Not into a smile, exactly. Into something like it. "You have had little cause to trust anyone at your back, Commander. Consider it a new experience."

He met her eyes, the faintest hint of tension in his jaw. "Trust is not a garment, Your Highness. It does not appear because someone ordered it."

They looked at each other for a heartbeat too long. Mira felt something sharp in the air between them. It was not attraction. It was not even open conflict. It was two people who understood they were bound together for reasons neither controlled.

Selene looked away first. Her gaze went back to the garment. "I want to see how it responds to proximity."

She stepped closer to Kael.

Mira felt the enchantment flinch.

The seam along his chest tightened, not enough to constrict his breathing, but enough for him to notice. He shifted, drawing in a slightly sharper breath. The collar warmed. The protective lines flared against the side facing Selene, as if interposing themselves. It was instinctive, not measured. A reaction to something the magic could not name.

Selene paused. Her eyes sharpened. "Did you feel that?"

Kael's attention cut to her. "Yes."

She looked at Mira. "Explain."

Mira stepped forward, heart pounding. She rested two fingers lightly on the shoulder seam, as if checking the fit. Her magic reached in, trying to soothe the defensive surge.

"The protective layer responded to a perceived shift in external focus," she said. It was technically true. The garment did not know Selene from a threat. It only knew approach. "It stabilized itself. With more reinforcement, I can teach it to differentiate between neutral proximity and actual danger."

Selene watched her. "Can you."

"Yes," Mira said quietly.

"Do that," Selene answered. "The garment will be useless if it treats its future queen as an attacker."

Mira nodded quickly. "Of course, Your Highness."

Kael spoke, voice mild. "Perhaps it is responding to intent rather than title."

Selene turned to him. "Do you suggest my intent is hostile, Commander?"

His expression did not change. "I suggest your concern for security is strong enough to make a garment wary."

The tension in the room thickened. Iris shifted her weight, ready to intervene if needed. The guards near the door looked as though they wished to be invisible.

Selene held Kael's gaze for a long moment. Then she stepped back, just enough for the fabric to ease. "I am concerned that our enemies may see this ceremony as an opportunity," she said. "If the enchantment believes I am an enemy, I question the seamstress's focus."

Mira felt heat rise under her skin. "Your Highness, the enchantment follows patterns of movement and emotion. It does not distinguish identity until the final stages. I have not bound it to any one person. It is still centering itself."

Selene's attention cut to her. "You are certain of that."

"Yes," Mira said. She lowered her eyes, then forced herself to lift them again. "My loyalty is to the success of this ritual and to the stability of the kingdom. I would not let the garment favor anyone in a way that endangers that."

"Even if that person stood in front of you," Selene said quietly. "Even if they confided in you."

Mira's breath stalled. The question carried more than curiosity now. It carried accusation veiled inside logic.

Kael glanced at Mira. She felt his gaze like a physical weight, but she did not look back. If she did, Selene would see too much.

"We have not spoken beyond what is required for fittings," Mira said, which was technically true, even if the content of those required conversations had skimmed dangerous depths.

"Have you met him before this commission?" Selene asked. Her voice remained calm. "Outside this room. Outside the palace."

The tent. The blood. The desperate pulse beneath her fingers.

"No," Mira said.

The lie tasted like iron. She kept her face as steady as she could. If Selene caught the slight hitch in her voice, she gave no sign, but her eyes narrowed a trace.

Kael's gaze lingered on Mira a second longer, then turned back to Selene. "Is this interrogation part of the ceremony, Your Highness, or a new form of entertainment?"

Selene offered him that small almost smile again. "I am making sure the cloth that binds us does not decide to choose sides before we even stand together."

"The cloth does not choose," Kael said. "People do."

Her attention slid back to Mira. "Exactly."

The rest of the fitting proceeded in brittle silence. Mira adjusted the hem, checked movement at the elbows, marked the places where the garment needed more space to accommodate armor beneath. Kael complied with each request. He lifted his arms. Turned. Sat and stood. He did everything she asked without complaint, but his body language had withdrawn. He had tucked himself behind the same careful walls he wore in council rooms.

Selene watched every small interaction. Every time Mira reached for a seam near his shoulder, Selene's eyes followed. When Mira stepped a fraction closer than strictly necessary to check the hang of cloth at his back, Selene noticed that distance too. It was not jealousy.

It was calculation. She was measuring something Mira could not risk naming.

Once Mira finished, she stepped back. "That is all I need for now," she said softly. "I will reinforce the enchantments and adjust response sensitivity before the next fitting."

"See that you do," Selene replied.

Kael began to remove the garment. He unfastened the closures, then shrugged out of it. As he did, the fabric clung for an instant longer along his shoulders, as if reluctant to let go. Mira saw it. She hoped no one else did.

Selene's gaze flicked down. Her eyes tightened. She saw.

Mira accepted the garment from Kael and folded it across her arms. Her fingers pressed into the silk harder than necessary. Her magic murmured in her bones, unsettled.

Kael put his coat back on. He fastened the buttons with precise motions, then looked toward Selene. "Will there be anything else, Your Highness?"

"For now, no," she said. "You may go."

He nodded. Before he turned away, his gaze brushed past Mira one last time. There was no smile, no frown. Only a question he did not ask.

Then he left, taking his guards with him.

The room changed the moment the door closed. It felt thinner, as if something essential had been removed.

Iris waited by the window, hands folded. The guard at the door remained stone faced. Selene, however, did not leave.

She stepped closer to the table again. "Put the garment down," she told Mira.

Mira obeyed. She laid the garment flat. Her pulse beat in her throat.

Selene reached out and placed her hand on the collar. This time, she did not touch lightly. Her palm pressed against the seam with clear intent.

The enchantment flared.

Not violently, but unmistakably. The threads stiffened under her hand, reinforcing the side facing Kael's former position. Even with him gone, the garment knew where he had been. It braced.

Selene's expression did not change, but something in her eyes cooled further. She removed her hand slowly.

"You insist the enchantment is not personal," she said. "Yet it reacts to him and resists me. Explain that."

Mira's mouth felt dry. "The garment recognizes pressure and intention. The Commander carries an unusual presence. His history has likely impressed itself on the cloth. Your Highness brings a different kind of force. It may interpret that as information it must adjust to."

"Interesting," Selene said. "You speak as if it has thoughts."

"Not thoughts," Mira said. "Patterns. It follows the strongest pattern it senses. He is a soldier. You are a ruler. The magic may be reading the contrasts. I can rebalance it."

Selene watched her in silence for several heartbeats. Mira felt each one.

"Tell me honestly, Seamstress," Selene said at last. "If the moment came when the garment had to choose between shielding the man or preserving the exact shape of the ritual, do you believe it would protect him."

Mira did not answer. She could not answer without betraying something. Silence formed a tight band around her chest.

Selene saw that silence. She studied it the way Kael might study an opponent's stance.

"You hesitate," Selene said softly. "That tells me more than lies ever could."

"My work is to prevent such a choice from existing," Mira managed. Her voice sounded rough in her own ears. "If the enchantment is balanced correctly, it will protect the ritual by protecting those within it."

"Spoken like someone who wants to save everything," Selene said. "That is rarely possible."

She looked down at the garment. "You care what happens to him."

Mira's pulse hammered. "My duty is to your union, Your Highness."

"That is not what I asked," Selene said.

She stepped closer, close enough that Mira could see the fine line at the corner of her eye where strain had etched itself. "You have feelings about the Commander. Perhaps admiration. Perhaps fear. Perhaps something else. I do not require the exact shape, only the truth that they exist."

Every part of Mira screamed to stay quiet.

"I am a seamstress," she said. "My feelings do not matter."

"You are an enchanter," Selene corrected. "Your feelings matter very much. Magic listens to the heart that guides it. That is why I wanted someone quiet. I assumed quiet meant simple. It appears I was mistaken."

The words stung in a way Mira had not expected.

"I assure you," Mira said, struggling to keep her voice even, "I am not foolish enough to let my heart interfere with a royal commission."

Selene held her gaze. "I believe you intend that. Intent is not always enough to stop what lives beneath it."

She let that settle in the air before continuing. "Understand this, Mira Nerielle. If this garment fails to perform as required, if it chooses him over the rite or me over him or any imbalance of that sort, the palace will not blame the cloth. They will blame you."

Mira felt the warning like ice in her veins. "I understand."

"If you find that your work is becoming too personal," Selene said, "you will inform Steward Merrow. We can replace you before the problem becomes irreversible."

The terror at that thought surprised Mira. Someone else weaving the cloth. Someone else touching the same silk, hearing his voice, feeling the way his presence shifted the enchantment. Part of her revolted at the idea with a force that startled her.

Selene saw the flicker of something on her face. She gave a tiny, cool smile.

"Yes," she said softly. "That is what I thought."

She turned to go, then paused at the doorway.

"One more thing," Selene said. "There are many ways to serve the kingdom. Some people do it with their lives. Some with their silence. Some with their honesty." She regarded Mira with that pale, measuring gaze. "Decide which you are before this ceremony ends."

She left without waiting for a reply. Iris followed her after a brief, apologetic glance toward Mira.

When the door closed, the room exhaled.

Mira stood there, hands resting on the edge of the table, fingers digging into the wood. Her knees felt unsteady. Her breath came shallow and quick.

Selene knew.

Not everything. Not the battlefield. Not the blood. But enough. She knew that the magic was leaning. She knew that Mira's composure was not emptiness. She suspected that something more than professional duty tied Mira to the man who would wear this garment.

Mira looked at the cloth.

It lay still, quiet, no visible ripple of enchantment. Anyone else would see only silk. She saw the faint echo of his presence, stitched into seams through every moment they had shared the same air.

"You are going to get us both killed," she whispered to the garment, to her own magic, to the part of her that could not stop caring.

Her magic hummed in response. Not in words. In feeling. It held the shape of him, the weight of his exhaustion, the truth of his fear about being used until nothing of himself remained.

She sank into her chair, elbows on the table, hands covering her face. For a few breaths, she let herself feel the full weight of it.

If she tried to pull all that connection out of the cloth now, she might tear the enchantment apart. If she left it as it was, Selene would keep watching, keep testing, keep narrowing in on the vulnerability she had almost named.

The princess was not cruel. She did not need cruelty. She had clarity, ambition and a mind sharp enough to use any thread she could grasp.

Kael sensed that, even if he did not see every part. Mira had watched the way his shoulders tightened when Selene spoke of trust as something the garment could grant. He knew there was more to this marriage than peace.

Mira dropped her hands and stared at the collar.

Selene suspected a personal bond between them. That suspicion would not fade. It would grow. It might even be correct, if someone decided that saving a dying man created a thread that could not be cut.

Mira reached out and laid her fingers gently on the seam. The fabric warmed beneath her touch.

"I need you to stand for the rite," she said softly. "Not for him. Not for her. For the people who will believe in this ceremony."

Her magic stirred, uncertain.

"And if something must break," she whispered, "I would rather it be me than either of them."

The garment did not answer. It simply held the echoes of everything she had stitched into it and everything she was trying not to admit.

Outside, the rain began to fall harder again, as if the sky had decided to stop pretending it could hold anything back.

7

ira waited until evening to begin.

The palace lights burned low, and the rain had finally softened into mist that clung to the garden stones outside her window. Night offered privacy. Night offered space to think without the memory of Selene's eyes on the back of her neck. Most importantly, night offered the illusion that if something went wrong, no one would see.

She lit only one lamp.

Its warm glow brushed the edges of the room but left shadows heavy in corners. The garment lay across her table like an accusation. Pale silk and golden stitching, looking so innocent under low light. Nothing about it revealed the way it had reacted that morning, stiffening defensively against its future queen. Nothing revealed the pulse she had felt inside it.

If someone else touched it now, they might feel nothing at all. To anyone without magic, it was only cloth.

But Mira felt it watching her.

She sat. Her hand trembled slightly as she picked up her needle. She forced her breath to slow before the thread could react. Calm was necessary. Precision was necessary. If she wavered even a little, she risked feeding the enchantment more emotion.

Emotion was damaging. Dangerous. No enchantment should be guided by it.

Mira knew how to weave magic into fabric. She had trained herself to do it quietly, subtly, invisible beneath the surface, the way a river carves stone without asking permission. She had never fought against her own intent before. She had never needed to.

Tonight, she would try something she should not have to do. She would try to shift the enchantment toward Selene.

Not away from Kael entirely. That was impossible now. The cloth had tasted him. It had felt his presence, his voice, the weight of him standing still while she worked. The thread had remembered what she had tried to forget.

But if she could widen the enchantment's loyalty, it might at least stop resisting the princess. It might behave like a ritual garment, not a personal shield.

Mira pressed one palm flat to the table, grounding herself. She steadied the flow of magic in her chest until she felt it soften. She imagined pouring it like water into a new direction. Toward unity, not attachment. Toward purpose, not person.

She threaded her needle carefully. The thread was fine, half gold, half orchard silk. It shimmered faintly, responding to the lamp's light as if it held dawn inside it.

She guided it into the cloth, beginning a fresh seam along the inner channel. This was where the binding would flow during the ceremony. The seam would help decide how loyalty formed between Kael and Selene. If it leaned too strongly toward him, the garment might reinforce his protection while neglecting its role in the union. If it leaned toward her, it might restrict him instead.

Balance. Mira needed balance.

She whispered under her breath, barely audible, weaving thought into stitch.

"For the crown. For the kingdom. For the unity of two paths."

She closed her eyes briefly, focusing only on Selene. On the princess's strength. Her clarity. Her ambition. Her ability to hold a kingdom steady. She tried to respect those qualities, not fear them.

The garment warmed.

Relief stirred in her. She continued stitching. Her magic slid into the fabric, trying to create a channel that recognized the princess's authority as something to honor, not resist. She fed admiration into the thread, not attachment.

A sound echoed faintly in the hall. Mira's hand tightened. She paused, listening for footsteps. None came. The palace often whispered with movement at night. She had learned not to expect answers to every sound.

She returned to her work.

Slowly, carefully, she placed another stitch and another, guiding magic toward a different signature. She pictured Selene's presence, her cool eyes, her unwavering logic. She pictured the role Selene would soon take, not as a bride but as a political linchpin.

The garment warmed again, deeper this time. The seam pulsed faintly beneath her fingers.

Yes. It was accepting.

Mira sighed with relief, shoulders relaxing. She stitched faster now, trying to strengthen the connection to Selene before the cloth could resist.

She worked for nearly half an hour before she sensed something shift.

A tug.

Not physical, but magical, like a pulled thread inside her own chest. The garment stopped warming. It began to cool. Not cold, but hesitant.

She slowed her needle. "Stay with me. This is correct. This is what you must do."

The fabric stiffened slightly. The magic inside it recoiled, like a child refusing a spoonful of medicine. Mira frowned.

"You cannot choose," she whispered. "You must serve them both."

Her magic pulled harder this time. It did not want to move in the direction she pushed it. It refused.

She guided the needle again, firm but gentle. She pressed the thread into the seam, forcing the enchantment to align with Selene. She poured every bit of certainty she could muster into the cloth.

Respect her, she told it silently. Recognize her authority.

Instead, it bristled.

Mira felt a tremor along the collar. A faint tightening around the chest seam. As if the garment were bracing itself again, wary and protective.

She gritted her teeth. "Do not defy the ritual. It is not meant for one person. It is meant for the crown."

The magic pulsed sharply. Mira felt it against her fingertips, like a heartbeat rejecting her command.

Her frustration rose. She forced the needle through the cloth, guided magic harder, trying to direct it toward Selene's strength.

The fabric resisted.

It pulled back. Not violently but stubbornly. The magic refused to attach. Every push she made redirected itself, bending back toward Kael. Mira's palms dampened with stress. She wiped them against her apron, then braced herself and tried again.

"Listen to me," she whispered, her voice shaking. "You cannot protect him alone. He cannot bear it alone."

She pushed the thread harder.

Something snapped.

Not the needle. Not the cloth. Something inside the enchantment.

The garment surged.

The thread tightened suddenly around her fingers. It looped, twisted, coiled around her skin with a speed she had never felt. The lace pulled itself tight across her hand, constricting, pressing into her flesh.

Mira gasped and tried to pull back, but the thread held firm, winding around her finger like a living thing. The pressure deepened. The silk cut into skin. Sharp pain blossomed. A bead of blood formed, then more.

"Let go," she whispered, half command, half plea.

The lace did not obey. It clung tighter, almost gently. It squeezed with a slow squeeze, not to injure, but to mark her. As if claiming.

Blood welled around the thread.

Her magic burst in response, uncontrolled. It flowed into the cloth through the cut. Not forced in, not stolen, but offered. Mira's breath caught as the fabric drank it in.

Not greedily.

Reverently.

She felt the garment absorb her blood like a secret, sealing it into the weave. The cotton of her apron brushed her knee, yet felt worlds away. She could not move until the cloth decided to loosen.

It did, eventually, slackening its grip one thread at a time. The lace released her finger, leaving a deep, thin cut across the top where the thread had pressed.

Mira stared at her trembling hand. She wiped the blood quickly, but she knew it was too late. The garment had drawn it. Taken it. Kept it.

She pressed the wound with a cloth, heart hammering. Her fingers tingled with lingering magic.

"You cannot choose him," she whispered to the garment. "He is not yours."

The cloth lay still.

Yet she felt the truth in her bones.

It had already chosen.

Mira's throat tightened. Anger rose, desperate and panicked. "I will not let you favor him. You are meant for the crown. You belong to both of them."

The garment pulsed.

A soft, defiant thrum.

Mira's voice shook. "Why? Why him?"

She knew the answer. She knew but she asked anyway, needing to speak the fear aloud.

The magic did not speak words, but she felt the response like an echo in her blood.

Because you do.

Mira's breath broke. Tears gathered at the edges of her eyes before she could stop them. She slammed her hand against her mouth to silence the sound building in her throat.

She had tried to hide it. She had tried to bury it. She had tried to treat him like a stranger.

But her magic knew what her mind refused.

She cared.

The garment only reflected that truth.

She wiped her eyes fiercely. She was not foolish enough to name her feelings. She did not want them. She did not want to care about someone she could never have, someone who belonged to duty, someone who would be bound by magic to another woman because the kingdom demanded it.

But wanting and feeling were not the same.

Her magic had never followed her reason. It followed her heart. It always had. And now she had stitched that heart into royal silk.

Mira pressed her wounded finger harder against the cloth, as if grounding herself in the pain. Her hand shook. "Listen to me. Even if you choose him, you still must protect the ceremony. You must protect her when she stands beside him. You cannot fail your purpose."

The garment did not pulse again, but warmth remained in the seam. Acceptance, not obedience. It would not abandon its protection of him. But it would not fight the ritual either.

She could guide it still. She could not redirect it, but she could broaden it. Not shift loyalty away from Kael, but teach it the necessity of protecting those around him.

She could not make it a garment for two.

She could make it a garment for all.

For the kingdom. For the crown. For the peace that was demanded.

Her magic could not be neutral, but it could be selfless.

Mira drew a deep breath. She steadied her hands and threaded a new length of silk. Not with the intent to change the garment's heart. But to widen the path through it.

She stitched into the seam carefully, letting her magic stretch outward. Not toward Selene as a person of power, but toward the idea of peace, the burden of unity, the protection of everyone who needed this marriage to succeed.

Her magic hesitated at first, confused by the unfamiliar concept. Unity was not a person. It was not someone to protect or love. But slowly, it recognized the shape she offered.

Not attachment.

Purpose.

The cloth warmed again as she wove that feeling through the channels, not replacing its loyalty, but expanding its duty.

Through hours of quiet stitching, her magic softened and stretched, like a ribbon pulled into a larger circle.

When dawn touched the edge of the sky, Mira stopped at last. She had not finished, but she had begun something new.

The garment now protected Kael because she cared for him.

It protected the others because she cared for him enough to protect them too.

Sacrifice, not neutrality.

It was not what Selene wanted. It was not what the council planned. But it might be the only version that would work.

Mira wrapped her wounded finger. She cleaned the last trace of blood from the thread. She whispered to the garment one last time before resting her head on her arms.

"You will keep them alive," she said. "You will keep him alive. And you will keep her safe beside him."

The enchantment pulsed faintly, warm and heavy, like an oath accepted.

Mira closed her eyes and slept at her worktable as the sun rose, unaware that she had just created a garment that would defy command, not through rebellion, but through protection so fierce it would not allow the kingdom to break the very man it sought to bind.

She had not diverted its loyalty.

She had turned it into a shield for more than one life.

And in doing so, she had sealed her fate with every stitch.

8

———

The day after the lace drew her blood, Mira moved like someone who had misplaced a piece of herself and refused to admit it.

Her finger throbbed beneath its bandage. The cut was not deep, but it pulsed in time with her heartbeat, a steady reminder of the moment the garment had claimed her. Every time she flexed her hand, she felt the ghost of the lace around her skin, tightening, binding, refusing to let go.

She tried to work as if nothing had changed.

The palace did not pause to ask if an artisan's magic had chosen a side. Servants still carried trays through narrow halls, guards still walked their routes, and somewhere above all that motion, nobles argued over maps and treaties while stewards like Iris Merrow tried to keep everything from falling apart.

Mira kept her head down and sewed.

The garment lay across the table, deceptively peaceful. The outer layer gleamed under the morning light, smooth and pale, the gold thread along the edges catching hints of brightness. The inner seams, the ones that mattered most, were mostly hidden now. Only she could feel what lived inside them.

She placed a reinforcing stitch along the waist seam, guiding her magic into a broad, even spread that would help distribute impact if the wearer was struck. She imagined arrows glancing away, blades catching on unseen resistance, force dispersing harmlessly. Her magic followed that thought, grateful for something simple.

She felt tired in a way that had nothing to do with muscles.

There was a knock on the door. A light one. Polite.

Mira looked up. "Enter."

The door opened. Iris Merrow stepped inside. Her expression held its usual calm, but her hands were clasped more tightly than usual in front of her. Mira noticed the whiteness of her knuckles.

"Seamstress," Iris said. "You are summoned."

Mira straightened. "Summoned where."

"To a private audience with Her Highness." Iris did not bother with preamble. "Now."

Her stomach tightened. "I thought the next review would be during the fitting."

"This is separate," Iris said. "Bring your notes. Not the garment."

That was unusual. Selene did not like talking about theory without seeing results. Mira wiped her hands on her apron and reached for the folder where she kept her diagrams and written observations. The pages inside crackled softly as she picked it up.

Iris watched, eyes flicking briefly to the bandage on Mira's finger. She said nothing, but the glance told Mira she had noticed. Nothing escaped Iris Merrow for long.

"Is there a problem with the work," Mira asked.

"That is for Her Highness to explain," Iris said. "Walk with me."

Mira followed her out.

The corridor felt narrower today. The familiar stone walls, the framed tapestries that showed old battles and older legends, seemed to lean closer. Iris moved at a brisk pace without rushing, her steps carrying the certainty of someone who knew every hall in the palace by memory. Mira kept up in silence, clutching the folder to her chest.

They passed servants who lowered their gazes, guards who

nodded to Iris and gave Mira quick, curious glances. She ignored them all.

Iris led her not to the formal council chamber or the open receiving hall, but to a smaller side room near one of the inner courtyards. Mira had never been inside this one. The door was plain, the wood old and polished by years of use. No ornate carvings, no heraldry. It was a room for private matters.

Two guards stood outside. They stepped aside at Iris's approach. One opened the door for them.

"Only the seamstress," the guard said quietly. "Her Highness's instruction."

Iris gave Mira a brief look, a flash of something like sympathy passing through her eyes. "You will be respectful," she said. "And careful."

Mira nodded. Her throat felt dry. She stepped inside.

The door closed behind her with a soft but final sound.

The room was modest by royal standards. A single long window looked into an internal garden where light fell on damp stones and a bare-limbed tree. A table sat near the center with two chairs. There was no throne, no elevated seat. Only a simple setting, as if meant to disarm anyone who entered.

Princess Selene stood by the window.

She did not turn immediately when Mira entered. She watched the courtyard instead, the way a thin stream of water ran along the stones, guided by small carved channels. She wore a gown of soft gray today, nearly the color of the sky, with only a narrow belt of silver at her waist. Her hair was braided up and pinned with three small metal combs.

"Your Highness," Mira said, bowing her head.

Selene's reflection in the glass shifted. Then she turned.

"Seamstress," she said. "Come sit."

She gestured to the chair opposite the one she moved toward. Her tone was mild, polite, neither warm nor cold. That somehow made Mira more tense.

Mira crossed the room and sat, careful to keep her posture

straight. She set the folder on the table, hands resting lightly on top of it.

Selene sat as well. Up close, the faint shadows under her eyes were more visible today. She looked composed, but tired at the edges. A ruler who had been reading too many documents and sleeping too little.

For a few moments, she simply regarded Mira in silence.

"You have been working late," Selene said at last. "More than required."

Mira kept her gaze on the princess's face. "There is much to do before the ceremony. The enchantments require careful layering."

"You burned scrap cloth yesterday," Selene said. "Quite a lot of it, according to the steward who is responsible for waste." Her tone carried no accusation yet, only observation. "You have been experimenting."

Mira's fingers twitched on the folder. "I needed to test how the protection would behave when expanded. The ritual channels are complex. I wanted to avoid unforeseen reactions."

"Unforeseen reactions," Selene repeated softly. "Like resisting me while the Commander stands quietly and does as he is told."

Mira's breath caught. "The garment will not resist you when completed, Your Highness. I am correcting that."

"Are you." Selene's gaze was sharp but calm. "Tell me what you have done with the enchantment since our last meeting."

Mira swallowed. "I have tried to widen its focus. It reacted strongly to him at first. I am teaching it to recognize the ritual as a whole, not only the wearer. It will protect you when you stand beside him, not treat you as a threat."

"Not treat me as a threat," Selene repeated. "Such a modest goal."

Silence settled for a moment. The faint sound of courtyard water drifted in through the window.

"Open your folder," Selene said.

Mira did so, laying out the diagrams of seams and channels, her neat notes in the margins. She turned pages so that the princess could see the sections where she had written adjustments for balance and responsiveness.

Selene leaned forward, scanning the ink. "Your handwriting is precise," she murmured. "It matches your stitching."

"Thank you, Your Highness."

"It was not a compliment," Selene said. "Merely an acknowledgment of fact. You have a meticulous mind. It would be a waste to keep you in a corner of the atelier forever."

Mira did not know what to say to that. She stayed quiet.

Selene tapped a finger next to a particular line of script. "Here. Where you wrote that you had difficulty redirecting the enchantment toward my presence. Explain this difficulty."

Mira's chest tightened. She chose her words with care. "The enchantment bonded strongly to the Commander during the first fittings. His life carries a force that affected the cloth. My magic follows patterns of presence. Once it recognized him, it anchored to that recognition. Redirecting it is not simple."

"And why does it anchor to him so strongly," Selene asked. "Is it only his nature, or your attention."

Mira forced herself to breathe evenly. "He is a man who has survived many battles. The weight of those experiences shapes him. The cloth feels that. My magic reacts to it."

Selene watched her closely. "Only that."

Mira held her gaze. "Yes, Your Highness."

A beat of quiet passed, heavy but not yet crushing. Then Selene sat back in her chair. Her posture relaxed, hands folding neatly in her lap.

"Very well," she said. "Let us speak plainly."

Mira did not relax. Plain speech from a princess was rarely simple.

"This marriage is not only about peace," Selene said. "I told you that before. It is a tool. A symbol. A guarantee. But there is more."

Her tone shifted slightly, a fraction less formal. "My father's health is failing. The council is divided. Some trust me. Some do not. They trust him even less. They see him as necessary and dangerous. A blade they cannot put down and do not know how to sheathe."

Her gray eyes held Mira's. "If we are bound, their fear becomes softer. They will believe that through me, they can reach him. That through the ritual, he is less likely to become something uncontrollable."

Mira heard the unspoken parts. A controlled weapon was useful. An uncontrolled one was terrifying.

She said carefully, "The enchantment is meant to reinforce that bond."

"Yes." Selene's fingers tightened slightly together, a small sign of strain. "But what they do not fully understand yet is how deep that bond will go."

Mira's heart picked up speed. "Your Highness."

Selene lifted a hand, palm facing up. "You saw the note about blood contact. That is only part of it. The rite does more than solidify loyalty. It shares weight."

Mira forced herself to ask. "What kind of weight."

Selene studied her as if measuring whether she could handle the answer. "Pain," she said simply. "The ritual ties our suffering together. If he is wounded, I will feel it. If I am harmed, he will feel it. Not in equal measure perhaps, but enough."

Mira's skin prickled. "That is dangerous."

"That is the point," Selene said quietly. "If someone wishes to hurt him, they must be willing to hurt me. If they wish to hurt me, they must accept that he will know, that he will share it. It makes casual cruelty inconvenient. It also makes betrayal costly."

Mira thought of Kael's words. I am afraid of becoming something that has no place beyond duty. He already carried a burden heavy enough to crush someone less strong. Now they wanted to stitch another weight on him. One he had not chosen.

She took a careful breath. "Does he know."

Selene's eyes flickered. "He knows there will be a binding. He knows there will be blood contact. He does not know the full depth of the sharing."

"That seems," Mira began, then stopped. The word cruel hovered, dangerous and foolish.

"Unwise," she said instead.

Selene's mouth curved into something that was almost a smile. "You choose your words carefully. Good."

Mira pressed her palm against the edge of the table to steady herself. "You want the enchantment to strengthen that sharing."

"Yes," Selene said. She did not hide it, did not pretend otherwise. "I want the bond to be unbreakable. If we are to stand together before the kingdom, I want no doubt in anyone's mind that we are tied. His strength, my position. Our pain. All of it."

Mira imagined it, for a moment. A blade striking him, the same flare of pain echoing in Selene's chest. A poison slipped into Selene's cup, sending weakness into Kael's limbs. A world where any attempt to hurt one of them spread that hurt. It would deter enemies. It would also trap them both.

"How much sharing do you want," Mira asked quietly. "There are degrees. A light echo, a mirrored sensation, a full transfer."

Selene's gaze cooled. "You know more about shared burden rites than someone at your station should."

Mira did not flinch. "I have read. I like to understand what my hands are making."

"Good," Selene said again, though the word tasted different now. "Then you understand the power in it. If the bond is light, it can be ignored. If it is strong, it can save lives."

"It can also destroy," Mira said before she could stop herself.

Selene's expression did not change, but her eyes hardened slightly. "Only if someone chooses to break it."

She looked down at the diagrams again. "I want the bond closer to the second level. More than a faint echo. Less than complete transfer. Enough that neither of us can claim ignorance of the other's suffering. Enough that if the council thinks to use him as a blunt instrument, they remember that any injury he takes will reach the person they expect to remain untouched."

There was a strange kind of fairness in that. Twisted, but real. The king's council liked wars carried out by other people's bodies. This would make that harder.

At the same time, it meant Kael would no longer be able to take a blow without dragging her into it too. He would hesitate more. He would pay a price every time he used his own body as a shield.

Mira sat very still. "You want to share his pain."

"For the sake of the kingdom, yes," Selene said. "For my own sake, also yes. It gives me leverage. It keeps him from being sent into hopeless battles when those above him have grown too fond of glory."

"Does he have a choice," Mira asked, unable to leave that question unspoken.

Selene's lips flattened. "No more than I do."

Mira believed that partly. The princess was bound by duty in her own way. Yet Selene had more room to decide how to use that duty.

"I am telling you this," Selene continued, "because the depth of the sharing depends on your work. The garment carries the initial flow. The blood on the cloth will follow the paths you have prepared. If you sew for a light echo, that is what we will have. If you sew for a stronger tie, the ritual will deepen it."

She looked directly at Mira. "I want it deep."

There it was. The real reason for this private summons.

Selene leaned back slightly. "If you do as I ask, if you strengthen the bond beyond what is strictly required, I will see that you are rewarded when this is over."

Mira's pulse thundered. "Rewarded how."

Selene did not hesitate. "You will not return to the back of the atelier. You will have your own workshop, not in the servant quarters, but in the artisan district near the palace. You will have apprentices, assistants, your own seal. Your name will appear on royal commissions. You will no longer be the quiet girl fixing sleeves in the corner."

Mira swallowed. Images flickered, quick and unhelpful. A room of her own that was permanent, not borrowed. Tools she could choose. Younger seamstresses learning under her direction, not ignoring her presence. A life that did not require hiding her talent.

Selene continued, voice smooth. "You will be granted a stipend sufficient to move out of the servant housing. You would be able to choose where to live, within reason. Safety within the city walls. Protection under my name."

Mira thought of her small rented room with its cracked window-pane and thin blanket. The way the draft slipped through the wall in winter. The worry each month about whether she could pay for both food and thread.

All of that could change.

Selene's gaze sharpened. "You hesitate, so let me be more pointed. If you do this, I will ensure that no one in this palace ever uses your magic without your consent. You will be under my protection. Not the council's. Not the king's. Mine."

Mira's heart stumbled.

For someone like her, an unregistered enchanter, that meant everything. The worst of her fears had always been that someone would discover her ability and decide it belonged to them. That she would be taken from her quiet work and forced to weave weapons or cages. Selene was offering a shield against that future.

At a price.

Mira looked down at her hands. Her bandaged finger rested against the wood. The cut throbbed gently, as if reminding her of what she belonged to already.

"To deepen the bond," Mira asked, voice barely above a whisper, "what exactly must I do."

Selene did not miss the shift in her tone. Her eyes cooled further, knowing she was close to winning something.

"You will strengthen the channels that connect the heart seams," Selene said. "Not only for one direction, but both. You will reinforce the pathways that read internal state. Pain, fear, strain. The garment will carry that information both ways more intensely."

Mira pictured it. Every time Kael took a blow, Selene would feel the echo in her chest. Every time Selene was threatened, Kael would feel a flare of warning. They would become mirrors of harm.

"What about joy," Mira asked before she could stop herself.

Selene blinked. "Joy."

"Yes," Mira said, surprising herself with her own insistence. "Shared burden rites often amplify other sensations. Relief. Comfort.

Warmth. If you deepen the channel for pain, you might also deepen the one for its absence."

Selene considered that. "I had not thought much about joy."

Of course not.

"But you are correct," Selene said. "If the flow is strong, it will carry all things. Perhaps that is no bad thing. The Commander is not familiar with peace. If he feels it in me, it may help."

Mira doubted Selene held much peace inside her, but she did not say so. She listened as the princess laid the trap more carefully.

"You are not a fool," Selene said. "You know that I am asking you to do something that carries weight. Something that might cost him. It will cost me too. I am not pretending otherwise."

She leaned forward, elbows resting lightly on the table. "But tell me this, Mira Nerielle. Is it more cruel to let him continue as he is, bearing every blow alone, or to bind someone to share it with him."

"He did not agree to share it," Mira said.

"He agreed to the ritual," Selene replied. "He knows bindings come with cost. We both step into this with our eyes open enough."

Enough. Not fully.

"If he refuses later," Mira said, "after learning the truth."

Selene's mouth thinned. "He will not refuse. There would be no war if refusal solved anything. He will see that this protects more people than it hurts."

Mira thought of Kael's quiet words in the workroom, his fear of becoming nothing but duty. Of being used without end. This binding would add another layer. It would give him access to Selene's pain, yes, but it would also ensure that he could never take a wound without dragging her into it.

She struggled with that picture. It was both protective and cruel. Both mercy and weapon.

"You want him unable to sacrifice himself easily," Mira said slowly. "You want to make sure he cannot take reckless risks for the crown without thinking of you."

"Yes," Selene said. "If he must think of me, he will also think of the kingdom. I am not separate from it. The council forgets that sometimes. They think of me as ornamental. This will remind them otherwise."

She tilted her head slightly. "So. You understand the work now. You understand what I ask. I offer you advancement, wealth, safety, a place where your magic is honored instead of hidden. In return, you strengthen the ritual. You make the bond deep."

Silence expanded between them.

Mira's mind raced and stilled at the same time. Advancement. Wealth. Protection. Her entire life shifting into something less fragile, less invisible. No more scraping coins, no more fear that someone would drag her to a cold chamber and demand she sew cages around people's minds.

At the same time, her stitches would carve a new burden into Kael's life. Every cut, every broken bone, every ache would no longer end at his skin. It would echo into someone else. Into Selene.

Part of her thought, perhaps that was right. He carried too much alone. Another part whispered that he had not been asked. That binding someone's pain to another person without full knowledge was wrong.

Selene watched her wrestle with it, patient and quiet.

"If I refuse," Mira asked, "what happens."

Selene's face did not harden, but a small stillness settled into it. "If you refuse, you will still complete the garment at the level already agreed. I am not ordering you to disobey your conscience. I am offering you a choice."

That sounded too generous. Mira waited.

"However," Selene continued, "if you refuse, I cannot guarantee you the protections I described. You will finish this commission as expected. You will be paid your standard fee. Then you will return to your old life. Whatever attention your magic has attracted will belong to others to decide."

There it was.

Not a direct threat. Simply a reminder. Selene could shield her from the hungry eyes that might look at her work and think of other uses. Or she could step aside and let the council decide what to do with a seamstress whose enchantments nearly rejected a princess for a general's sake.

Refusing was not safe.

Accepting would betray something she had not even dared to name fully.

Mira thought of her parents, long gone, who had died before they could see the palace from afar. Of her cousin who had taken her to the war camp that night. Of the wounded soldier she had saved without expecting anything in return.

She thought of Kael's shoulders easing when she told him to relax, of his voice when he admitted he feared being nothing but duty. She thought of how the garment had tightened around him when her magic reacted.

She thought of Selene, who was neither villain nor savior, but something more complicated. A ruler who would share pain if it meant keeping control of a kingdom intact.

"What you ask," Mira said at last, voice thin and steady, "is not a small thing."

"I know," Selene said.

"I do not want to see him break under the weight of it," Mira continued.

"Neither do I," Selene replied. "You think I want to be dragged down by every wound he takes. I do not. But I would rather bear it than let him stand alone. This way, if the council tries to throw him into endless violence, they must consider that it will strike me too. It gives me leverage to keep him out of needless slaughter."

"Or to keep him in line," Mira said before her caution caught up.

Selene's eyes flashed briefly. Then she nodded. "Yes. That too. And perhaps he needs that. The world has trusted his judgment with too much blood."

Mira did not know if she agreed. She did and did not, all at once.

"You care for him," Selene said quietly. The calm observation cut through Mira's thoughts. "You may not name it. You may even resent it. But you do. That is why you hesitate."

Mira's heart lurched. "I care about what is done to him."

"And to you," Selene added. "You are part of this. Do not pretend otherwise. Your blood is in that garment now."

Mira flinched.

"Do not look so startled," Selene said. "Did you think I would not feel the shift yesterday. The magic changed. It settled in a new way. You carry the mark of it on your hand."

Her gaze dropped to the bandaged finger. Mira curled her hand into a fist.

"I do not know the exact shape of what happened," Selene said. "But I know that your bond to that cloth changed. Which means your bond to him did too. You are already entangled. This bargain only decides how you use that entanglement."

The room felt too small.

Mira wanted to stand, to pace, to breathe air that did not feel so loaded. She stayed still.

"You do not have to answer now," Selene said at last. "Think on it. But do not think long. The final layers must be woven soon. The ritual cannot wait."

She rose. Mira did too, automatically.

Selene looked at her one more time. "You want to protect him. I want to protect the kingdom. Those desires do not have to be enemies."

"And if they become enemies," Mira asked quietly.

Selene considered her. "Then you will have to decide which one you are willing to live without."

She walked to the door, hand on the handle. Before she opened it, she added without turning, "Advancement, wealth, safety. Or a clear conscience that might not keep you, or him, alive."

Then she left.

The door closed with a soft click.

Mira stood alone in the small room. The faint sound of water in the courtyard returned, steady and indifferent. It did not care what choices a seamstress made.

She sat slowly, as if her knees might not hold. Her hands shook when she tried to gather her notes. She pressed her palms flat on the table instead.

Advancement. Wealth. Protection.

She could have her own workshop. Her own seal. She could step out of the background and into a position where her work mattered openly. She could stop fearing that someone would drag her to a cell and demand her magic on their terms. Selene was right. Without protection, the council might see her as a resource to be used. With protection, she would have a shield.

But that shield would be built on deeper pain.

Mira imagined Kael realizing, too late, that every bruise he took, every bone that cracked, every blow meant not only his pain but Selene's. She imagined him hesitating in battle, forced to choose between saving someone and sparing her. She imagined his face when he learned that someone had made that choice for him.

If Mira did as Selene asked, she would be that someone.

Her hands curled slowly into fists.

If she refused, she might lose any chance to protect him from worse choices. Another enchanter, less careful, might be brought in. They might deepen the bond anyway, but without any thought for mercy. At least Mira cared. At least she would try to find a way to soften the edges.

She felt trapped.

Either path hurt him.

Either path tied her tighter to this ritual, to these people, to a life she had never wanted but could not escape.

She pressed her bandaged finger into the wood of the table until pain sharpened her focus. In that pain, she found a thin thread of certainty.

She could not decide for him. That felt wrong in her bones. Magic was her craft, but his body was his own.

Yet the choice Selene offered did not include his voice. People above him had already decided to bind his fate. The only place left for choice was in how much harm Mira allowed into the weaving.

She thought of sharing pain.

If she refused to strengthen the bond, he would remain alone. His wounds would be his own, but nothing would stop others from piling them on him. If she agreed, at least someone else would carry part of that burden, and those who sent him into danger might hesitate.

Selene's logic, cruel and clear, wrapped around Mira's thoughts.

After what felt like a long time, Mira stood. She gathered her folder to her chest and walked back to her workroom in a daze, Iris's curious glance bouncing off her like a dropped pin.

She closed the workroom door and leaned against it, chest tight.

The garment waited. Silent. Knowing.

She crossed the room and laid her palm on the collar. The cloth warmed immediately, as if greeting her. The enchantment thrummed softly, her magic and his presence intertwined.

"You heard," she whispered, as if the garment had ears. "Or you felt enough to guess."

It pulsed.

"Shared pain," Mira murmured. "Shared harm. We can make it light. We can make it heavy."

Her hand trembled. "She wants deep."

The garment did not respond in any clear way, but she felt its readiness. It would carry whatever she put into it. It did not care about politics. It cared about connection.

She closed her eyes.

"I will not make it cruel," she whispered. "Not if I can help it. If I must deepen the bond, I will temper it. I will lace comfort into it as well. If they must share pain, they will share strength too."

An idea pressed at the back of her mind. Dangerous. Possible.

She could widen the channels not just for hurt, but for resilience. For healing. She could teach the garment to not only carry the echo of wounds, but also to pass along warmth, steadiness, the feeling of standing instead of falling. If Kael was cut, Selene would feel it, yes, but she might also feel his refusal to break. If Selene faltered, he would feel her effort to stand, not only her fear.

She could build something that did not just punish. Something that refused to let either of them collapse easily.

It would still bind them against their full knowledge.

She hated that.

She loved that it might keep him alive.

Another choice, terrible and narrow, but a choice all the same.

"You will not be a chain," she told the garment under her breath. "You will be a bridge. If I do this, you will not drag them down. You will hold them up."

Her magic stirred at the idea. It liked paths, connections, shared burdens that did not exist to destroy. It could work with that.

So could she.

Her conscience screamed at the edges, telling her this was still wrong, that consent should matter, that love, however quiet, had no right to decide another person's pain.

Another part of her, the part that had watched him bleed, that had seen him nearly die on a cold field, whispered that if someone would decide this, it should be someone who did not want him broken.

It should be her.

Mira drew a long, shaking breath and made the smallest bargain she could live with.

She would strengthen the spell.

But not only with pain.

She would take Selene's offer and twist it as far toward mercy as she could, even if that line was thin. She would accept the advancement, the protection, because with those she might have enough power later to change things again, to shield others, to refuse future demands.

She would betray something inside her. She would also protect more lives than just her own.

It was not a clean choice.

It was the only one she saw.

Her voice came out quiet, but steady. "So be it."

The garment warmed under her hand, as if acknowledging a vow.

Mira picked up her needle. Her bandaged finger ached as she guided the thread. She began to deepen the channels the way Selene wanted, but with every stitch, she added something that had not been requested.

A path for shared strength. A path for shared hope. A path for stubbornness in the face of despair.

If they were going to feel each other's pain, then they would also feel each other's refusal to give in.

"I am sorry," she whispered, to Kael, to Selene, to herself. "I am so sorry."

The magic settled, accepting her apology without judgment. It did not care if she was right or wrong.

It only cared that she kept stitching.

9

The palace archives always smelled faintly of dust and ink and something older than both, a dry scent that reminded Mira of pressed flowers kept between pages too long. She had only been allowed here once before, under supervision, to reference a pattern book. That visit had been brief, controlled, watched.

Today, Iris unlocked the door herself and handed Mira a small, engraved token.

"For access," Iris said quietly. "The archivists know better than to question a marked guest. Show them this if they hesitate."

Mira turned the disk in her fingers. It was made of brass, worn smooth at the edges, stamped with the royal crest on one side and a series of numbers on the other.

"Is this necessary," she asked. "I only need to see the ritual notes for the ceremony. The ones already provided do not explain how the sharing works in detail."

"That is precisely why you are here," Iris said. "Her Highness has authorized a temporary widening of your clearance. Use it carefully. Do not touch anything you do not absolutely need."

Mira glanced at the solid wooden door of the archive, at the worn handle polished by decades of hands.

"Why now," she asked. "The ceremony is approaching. Are they not afraid I will learn too much."

"They are very aware that you already know more than most," Iris replied. "Better you have the correct texts than make guesses. Besides, you are already bound by oath. If you speak of what you see without permission, there will be consequences you do not want."

The way she said it held no threat of her own, only a reminder of the palace's nature.

"I understand," Mira said.

Iris studied her for a moment, eyes lingering again on the bandaged finger. "Do not get lost in there," she added more softly. "Some books have teeth."

Mira almost smiled. "I will be careful."

The corner of Iris's mouth twitched, then smoothed out again. She nodded to the guard posted nearby. He opened the archive door.

Cool air washed over Mira's face as she stepped inside. The sound of the door closing behind her cut off the muffled life of the palace outside. In here, everything was subdued. The light came from narrow windows high above and glass-covered lanterns set at intervals along the walls. Shelves climbed toward the ceiling, packed with leather-bound volumes, scrolls, boxes of flattened maps. Dust motes floated lazily, catching the light.

At a central desk, an older man with thinning hair and round spectacles looked up from a pile of parchment. His gaze sharpened when he saw the token in her hand.

"Business of the crown," he said, voice dry. "Very well. What do you require."

"I have been asked to review records of binding rites," Mira said, trying to keep her voice polite and neutral. "Specifically those involving shared sensation, and those performed on individuals whose abilities awakened through trauma, not birthright."

The archivist's eyebrows rose slightly. "A precise request."

"I was told the information is scattered," Mira said. "I do not want to waste time looking in the wrong places."

"There are no wrong places in the archives," he said. "Only shelves that will consume more of your years than you intend to give them."

Despite his words, there was no malice in his tone. He squinted at her token again, reading the number, then heaved himself up from the stool.

"Follow," he said.

She did, weaving between towering shelves as he led her into the older section of the room. The air grew cooler as they went, the smell of dust deeper here. As they turned a corner, the light dimmed, and the archivist lit a small hand lamp.

"Shared sensation rites are not common," he said. "They cause as many problems as they solve. Most records are theoretical. The practical ones are in restricted cabinets." He shot her a sideways look. "Which you now have access to, apparently."

They stopped at a row of locked cases. The wood here was darker, the glass thicker. The archivist took a key ring from his belt and unlocked the middle case. Inside, books lay flat instead of upright, each one bound with a strip of fabric. He set the lamp on a small table and drew out a volume wrapped in deep red cloth.

"This is a collection of rituals sanctioned by previous courts," he said. "Including several binding rites that used shared burden as a deterrent for betrayal. Do not tear the pages."

He placed the book on the table and opened it with care. Inside, the text was written in dense hand, lines of ink marching across yellowed paper. Diagrams of circles, lines and symbols accompanied the descriptions.

Mira leaned closer, her heart picking up with a mix of dread and curiosity.

"Here," the archivist said, tapping one section. "See these marks. This describes bonds forged between a sovereign and a chosen champion."

The words on the page blurred for a second before her eyes refocused. She read slowly, lips moving silently.

In times when a ruler relied upon a single warrior whose strength was feared by ally and enemy alike, a rite was designed to tether that strength to the sovereign's life. Through mutual blood and woven channels of sensation, the warrior's power was bound in part to the sovereign's will, while the sovereign accepted a portion of the warrior's pain.

Her skin prickled.

She read on.

The shared sensation served two purposes. Firstly, it prevented the ruler from treating the warrior as expendable, as any injury inflicted upon him would echo in the ruler's own flesh. Secondly, and more dangerously, it allowed the ruler to temper the warrior's battle state, to either call forth the heightened ferocity that arose from near-death awakening, or to dampen it when it threatened to spill beyond intended bounds.

Near-death awakening.

Mira's breath stalled. Her finger tightened on the edge of the page.

The archivist watched her impassively. "You understand the reference."

"Yes," Mira whispered.

She remembered the tent. The blood. The way his breath had been shallow, fading, then suddenly stronger after her magic poured into him. He had not been born with some ancient bloodline gift. Whatever extra strength he manifested in battle had come from surviving that moment on the edge of death.

The book's ink went on, merciless in its clarity.

In such cases, the warrior's abilities were bound not to the land nor to a line of heritage, but to the crisis that shaped him. His strength rode along channels of survival, sharpened by the memory of nearly dying. Through careful enchantment, those channels may be connected to the sovereign's body, ensuring that the sovereign may, through directed intent, either open the path fully or constrict it.

Mira forced her eyes to keep moving.

This practice was controversial even in its earliest uses. While it granted rulers a measure of control over dangerously awakened power, it risked the warrior's autonomy. Too strong a bond, and the warrior's free will in battle could be overridden by the sovereign's panic, ambitions or fear. Too weak a bond, and the shared pain lacked deterrent effect.

She swallowed hard. Her throat felt tight.

"May I ask," she said quietly, "how many times such rites were used."

The archivist shrugged one shoulder. "Hard to say. Records that survived have their gaps. But enough that the council remembers them when afraid."

He turned a few pages farther. "Here is one that concerns your particular interest."

He pointed to a passage that mentioned Varyn by name.

In the reign of King Theral of Varyn, a great commander arose whose skill on the field was unmatched, but whose methods unsettled the court. Having survived a grievous wound that should have killed him, his ferocity in subsequent battles increased beyond prior measure. The council, fearing eventual madness or rebellion, sanctioned a binding rite with the crown princess of that time.

Mira read more quickly now, heart racing.

The garment used in the rite was woven with channels of sensation and will. The warrior's battle rage, once awakened, could be damped by the sovereign's conscious choice to close the channel, while shared pain served as a reminder of their mutual interdependence. Over time, however, the warrior grew quieter, less inclined to act outside direct orders. His instincts no longer fully his own, his autonomy thinned.

Mira whispered, "What happened to him."

The archivist tilted his head, scanning ahead. "It says here that he died in service. On the field, of course. The princess survived him, though she bore lingering pain for years after, despite the bond supposedly ending with his death."

Her chest hurt.

The text had more to say.

It is advised that such rites be used sparingly, if at all. While effective in securing control, they risk turning a person into an extension of sovereign will, rather than a separate mind, thereby destabilizing the very trust they are meant to reinforce.

Mira's hand shook as she lifted it from the page.

She thought of the channels she had already sewn. The paths she was deepening under Selene's instruction. They did not just carry pain. They carried the pulse of Kael's awakened strength. His battle state. The part of him that rose when danger came, sharpened by the memory of nearly dying.

Her magic was building routes that could be used to temper that state, to open or close it.

She heard her own voice from days before, telling Selene it might carry joy as well. Shared warmth. Shared resilience. She had clung to that as justification.

Now she saw the trap more clearly.

"It binds more than pain," she said softly.

"Everything binds more than intended," the archivist replied. "That is the nature of magic. It listens too well."

"Does it mention," she asked, "what happens if the enchantment is attuned personally to the warrior first. Before the ritual."

The archivist gave her a sharp look over his glasses. "Attuned personally. You have been busy."

Mira pressed her lips together. She said nothing.

He sighed and flipped a few pages farther. "There is a brief note here. A caution, really."

He traced a line with one crooked finger.

If, prior to the rite, the garment or enchantment has been attuned strongly to the warrior by an artisan whose magic is bound by care or personal attachment, the risk of over control increases. The channels may give not only the sovereign access to the warrior's strength, but also to his most instinctive reactions. In worst cases, the warrior's body may move as an extension of the sovereign's fear, rather than his own judgment.

Her vision blurred.

She stepped back from the table.

"Careful," the archivist warned. "You look like you might be sick. If you feel faint, sit. Do not fall on the books."

Mira swallowed, fought down the nausea rising in her chest, and sat slowly. The chair creaked under her.

She had not only woven shared pain. She had woven pathways that could let Selene reach into the very thing that made Kael terrifying on a battlefield. His ability to move without hesitation, to read danger faster than thought, to choose when to leap forward and when to hold back. If the bond settled the way these texts described, Selene could damp that state if she panicked. She could also sharpen it beyond what was safe.

Her love - or whatever word her heart deserved - had made the cloth attuned to him first.

The garment trusted him. It trusted her. Now she was carving into it routes that would allow someone else to reach through that trust.

Her accidental magic could enslave him.

Mira pressed her fingertips hard against her eyes until bright spots flared behind them. She dropped her hands and looked at the text again, forcing herself to read even though it hurt.

"Is there any record of breaking such a bond," she asked. "Once forged."

The archivist pursed his lips. "Not exactly. There are partial severances, painful and often fatal. Some speak of weakening over time, if the sovereign chooses not to use the channels. But a complete, clean undoing?" He shook his head. "You bind lives at that level, girl. That is not done lightly, nor undone easily."

She flinched at the word girl, but did not correct him. "What about softening it. Changing the flow after the rite is complete."

"That would require access to both participants and to the original artifact," he said. "And a level of trust that rarely exists once people realize what has been done to them. In my experience, people who feel controlled do not calmly invite the person who did it to fix things."

He looked at her more closely. "You are paler than when you walked in. Perhaps that is enough reading for today."

Mira wanted to argue. To demand every scrap of information, no matter how grim. But the words on the page had already lodged in her mind with brutal clarity. More text would not soften them. It would only add weight.

"May I copy this section," she asked. "Or borrow it."

"You may not remove it from this room," he said firmly. "But you may make notes. No names. No direct references. Only principles. That is the rule."

She nodded and reached for the small notebook she carried in her satchel. Her hand shook as she wrote, paraphrasing the most critical pieces.

Shared burden as deterrent. Channels to awakened battle state. Sovereign influence over warrior's strength. Risk of overriding will if bond deepened. Attuned weaving from artisan connected by emotion increases that risk.

Every word felt like a stone added to her chest.

When she finished, her script was messier than usual. She closed the notebook carefully, as if it contained something poisonous.

"Thank you," she said to the archivist. "You have been very helpful."

He shrugged. "Knowledge is not kind or cruel. It simply is. What you do with it, that is where trouble begins."

She could not argue.

He wrapped the book in its red cloth again and slid it back into the cabinet, locking the glass door. The sound of the key turning felt final.

Mira left the archives on unsteady legs. The hall outside seemed too bright. She blinked as her eyes adjusted to the change. Iris waited near a column, arms folded.

"Well," Iris said, watching her face. "You look as if the books did, in fact, have teeth."

Mira let out a breath that might have been a laugh if it had not sounded so thin. "They bite deep."

Iris studied her, then nodded toward the servant stairwell. "Go back to your workroom. Do not speak of what you read in the hall. We can talk there, if you need."

They walked in silence.

When they reached the workroom, Iris locked the door behind them and turned, back against the wood. "Tell me. In broad strokes. Nothing that will get either of us dragged in front of the council if someone overhears."

Mira clutched her notebook. "The ritual used on him, on them, was used before. On another commander and princess. It bound not only their pain, but his awakened strength. The one he gained from almost dying. The sovereign could damp it or call it forth."

Iris's face tightened. "And the cost."

"He lost parts of himself," Mira said. Saying the words made her want to curl in on herself. "His instincts. His autonomy. He became quieter. More obedient. Less able to move outside orders. When he died, she lived. With pain that never fully faded."

Iris's gaze went to the garment on the table, then back to Mira. "Do you believe this ritual is the same."

"The patterns match," Mira said. "The shared burden. The use of a garment. The presence of awakened power. It is almost identical."

"And your enchantment," Iris pressed. "What does it do in this context."

Mira looked at the gown. Her throat burned. "It opens the path. I thought I was only deepening shared sensation. I see now I am giving her a handle. One she might use to pull him back when he goes too far. Or push him forward when he would rather not."

"You did not know," Iris said. Her voice softened slightly.

"I should have," Mira said. "I should have forced them to tell me everything before I started. I should have refused until they did."

"Would they have told you," Iris asked.

"No," Mira said.

Iris nodded. "Then blame them more than yourself."

"That does not unmake what I have done," Mira said.

They were both quiet for a moment.

"You have a choice," Iris said at last. "You can weaken what you are weaving. Make it as soft as possible. Or you can lean into it and try to steer it toward something less harmful. Neither is safe."

"Selene wants it strong," Mira said. "She offered me protection if I do it. Or nothing if I refuse."

"And what do you want," Iris asked quietly.

Mira thought of Kael, who had not asked for any of this. Of Selene, who had asked for more pain than anyone should willingly invite. Of herself, caught between them.

"I want him to live," she said. "I want her to live. I want the kingdom not to tear itself apart. I want my magic not to decide who belongs to whom."

"That is too many wants," Iris said gently. "The world rarely grants even one."

Mira gave a hollow sound that might have been a laugh.

"There is something I should tell you," Iris added after a moment. "Not as a steward, but as someone who has watched these halls longer than you have drawn breath."

Mira looked up.

"Power will bind him, with or without your help," Iris said. "If not through magic, then through duty, orders, politics. You did not put him in chains. The crown did that the day they raised him to glory. The best you can do is decide whether the chain cuts or holds."

Mira swallowed. "What if I do both."

"Then you are honest," Iris said. "Most chains do."

She pushed away from the door. "I cannot tell you what to do. I am not brave enough to bear that blame. But I will say this: if someone must sit at the crossroads of his fate and hers, better someone who cares than someone who does not."

She unlocked the door. "I will leave you to your thoughts. Do not stay in them too long. They are as dangerous as old books."

When she left, Mira almost called her back, wanting some kind of anchor. Instead, she let the door close.

The workroom felt too quiet.

Mira walked to the table and rested her hands on either side of the garment. The silk gleamed softly.

"You are not a mind," she whispered to it. "You are threads. You do not understand what they will do with you."

Her magic stirred under her skin, answering the familiar presence of the cloth. It did not feel guilty. It felt ready.

She opened her notebook and read over the notes she had taken. Words about control. About the awakened state brought on by surviving death. About how channels could allow someone else to grip that state, like a handle on a blade.

Her thoughts ran in circles.

If she refused to deepen the bond, the council might bring in someone else who would do it without any attempt at mercy. If she did it herself, at least she could try to build in limitations, to leave some part of him beyond anyone's reach.

Her magic, born from the night she saved him, had already wrapped itself around his survival. It had tied her to him, whether either of them wanted that or not.

She stared at the collar.

"If I do nothing, they will still use you," she told the garment softly. "If I sabotage you, the kingdom may fall into war. If I shape you carefully, I may still trap him."

The options felt like walking along the edge of a blade.

Her chest hurt. She pressed her hand over her heart, feeling the beat against her palm.

She remembered that night in the tent.

She had not seen a legend then. She had seen a man drowning in his own blood. Her magic had moved before her mind could catch up, terrified of losing someone who fought so hard to live. She had not thought of ritual or politics or chains. She had only thought, Not this one. Not like this.

That same part of her spoke now.

If the bond must exist, let it be shaped by someone who does not want him broken.

She drew in a slow breath. She picked up her needle.

With every stitch along the heart channel, she wove two intentions: to deepen the shared burden as required, and to leave his mind as free as she could manage.

She could not stop Selene from feeling his pain. She could not stop him from feeling hers. But she could shape the flow so that the strongest path ran through their awareness, not their reflexes. She could make it harder for panic to seize control.

She whispered quietly as she worked.

"You will feel each other. You will know each other are alive. You will not be able to lie about harm. But you will not be each other's puppet."

Her magic listened, hesitant, then followed.

She did not know if it was enough.

As she sewed, the wound on her finger ached in rhythm with her thoughts. Her blood in the cloth. Her heart in the seams. His life in the ritual.

Her accidental love had given the garment a loyalty that could be twisted into chains.

All she could do now was hope that the same love, stubborn and unwilling to see him crushed, could bend those chains toward something that resembled protection instead.

Whether she had that right, she did not know.

Whether she had a better choice, she could not see.

Outside, bells rang distantly, marking another hour gone.

Inside, Mira kept stitching, every pass of the needle an argument with fate, the kingdom and herself.

10

ira did not remember when she had last eaten.

The light outside had shifted from bright to dull and into that colorless gray that lived between afternoon and evening. She still sat at her table, the garment spread before her like a quiet accusation. Threads lay in careful coils. Needles rested where she had placed them. A basin of water on the side table had gone still and cold.

Her thoughts refused to follow the neat patterns she had drawn on paper. They wandered, looping back to the same point each time.

The ritual can bind his strength. Not just his pain. Not just their senses. His strength. The part of him that rose from the edge of death.

Her notes sat open in front of her. The ink had dried to a dull brown. She stared at the words and did not really see them. Her eyes burned. Her finger throbbed under the bandage. The cut had stopped bleeding hours ago, but she swore she could still feel the silk around it, constricting, claiming.

She tried to sew. She failed.

Every time she picked up her needle, her hand shook. The thread snagged. Her magic did not know whether to move forward or pull back. It hovered in her chest, restless and unsettled, like a bird that had flown into the wrong room and could not find the window.

The garment lay still. It did not pulse or flare. It waited.

She brought the needle to the fabric again, slow and deliberate. She knew what needed to be done. The channels had to be completed. The ceremony was coming whether she agreed with it or not. If the enchantment remained half finished, the rite would be unstable. That would put everyone at risk, not just Kael and Selene.

Her hand hovered above the seam meant for the heart.

She could not push the needle through.

Her vision blurred. She blinked and realized tears had gathered without her noticing. She wiped them away with the back of her wrist, frustrated.

Crying was useless. It solved nothing. It did not change what the archives had revealed. It did not dissuade the crown. It did not unbind the silk from her blood.

A sound drifted through the door from the hallway. Footsteps. More than one set. Voices low and indistinct. She barely registered them. There were always footsteps.

Then there was a pause.

Silence, right outside.

She looked up, frowning slightly.

The knock came, firm and controlled, not loud. The kind of knock from someone who knew they did not need to beg for entry.

Mira quickly wiped her eyes again, though she knew she could not erase the redness completely. She took a breath and tried to steady her voice.

"Enter," she called.

The door opened.

Commander Kael stood there.

He wore no formal coat this time. Only a dark shirt and plain trousers, as if he had shed ceremony on his way here. His hair was slightly out of place, as though he had run a hand through it more than once. A faint line of tiredness cut under his eyes. Behind him, two guards waited at their usual distance.

He looked past them into the room. His gaze found her immediately.

The moment his eyes met hers, the garment under her hands warmed.

She pressed her palms flat against the table to hide the reaction.

"Seamstress," he said.

"Commander." She hated that her voice sounded hoarse.

He glanced once over his shoulder at the guards. "Wait outside."

One of them shifted. "Sir, we were instructed to remain with you when you visit the workroom."

"I will remain in the workroom," Kael said. "You will remain outside."

Something in his tone left no room for argument. The guards exchanged a look, then stepped back. The door closed. For once, Mira found herself alone with him.

Her heart picked up speed in a way she did not appreciate.

"You are not scheduled for a fitting today," she said, because it was easier than asking why he was really here.

"No," he agreed.

Silence stretched for a heartbeat.

He moved farther into the room, gaze flicking to the table where the garment lay, then back to her face. His brow knit slightly.

"You are not well," he said.

Mira straightened, irritated with herself that he could see anything at all. "I am fine."

"You are lying." He said it plainly, without accusation. The way he might note that the sky was cloudy.

Her cheeks warmed. "I am tired. That is all."

He watched her for a long moment. She forced herself not to drop her gaze. Then he stepped closer to the table.

"The garment feels different," he said.

Mira swallowed. "Different how."

He reached out, not touching it yet, just holding his hand above the silk as if sensing heat. "Heavier. As if something inside it is listening more closely."

Her stomach twisted. Of course he would feel that. He lived in a body attuned to danger. Even without magic, he would sense a shift in weight he was meant to carry.

"I have been deepening the binding channels," she said, keeping her tone as flat as she could. "It was always going to feel stronger as the ceremony approached."

He looked at her again. "And that unsettles you."

She laughed once, but it came out short and brittle. "It should unsettle you."

"Perhaps it does," he said. "But I am used to being unsettled."

He stepped around the table, closing the distance between them. Not enough to be improper. Enough that she could see the faint stubble along his jaw and the pale scar crossing it. She noticed, for the first time, how his thumb drifted up to rest against that scar, pressing gently, as if grounding himself.

"You are not here for a fitting," she repeated quietly. "Why did you come."

He held her gaze. Whatever he had come for, it had not been decided lightly.

"I felt something," he said.

The words sent a chill along her spine.

"Felt what," she asked.

He hesitated, thumb still pressed against the scar. "I was in a council meeting earlier. They were arguing again. About territory, supply lines, whether my presence on the border would provoke or prevent war." His eyes darkened briefly. "I tried not to listen more than necessary."

Mira could imagine it. Men in embroidered coats speaking of lives as markers on a board. Voices rising, hands slamming tables, all over decisions that could spill blood far away.

"In the middle of it," he continued, "I had the sudden sense of someone trying not to drown."

She stared at him.

He looked almost apologetic. "It was not a clear feeling. Just an abrupt pull. Like a thread tightening."

Her hand went unconsciously to her bandaged finger. The cut pulsed as if in reaction.

"I thought at first it was my own mind rebelling," he said. "Then it did not fade. It tugged again. Not physical. Not pain. Something else." He studied her face. "When it did not pass, I found myself here."

"You felt me," she said. Her voice sounded very small.

"I do not know what I felt," he replied. "Only that whatever it was led me to your door."

The garment's warmth eased, as if a puzzle piece had found its place. The deepening channels she had sewn for shared burden were not yet fully active, but they were awake enough to let echoes slip through.

She should have expected this. She should have been more careful.

She looked away before he could read further into her expression. "You should not be here without reason the council would approve."

"The council does not approve much of what I do," he said. "That has never stopped me."

He moved closer to the table, resting his hands lightly on the edge. His fingers brushed against the silk. The enchantment stirred under his touch, eager as a dog recognizing its master.

Mira's chest tightened. "Do not."

He looked at her hand, not at the garment. "You are shaking."

"I told you. I am tired."

He did something then that startled her.

He stepped around the table so he stood beside her, not across from her. The small shift changed everything. They no longer faced each other like artisan and client. They faced the garment together, bodies almost aligned, shoulders a hand's breadth apart.

"What did you find in the archives," he asked.

Her breath stopped.

"I found pattern notes," she said. "Old records of similar rites."

"You look as if those notes struck you," he answered. "Hard."

She could not deny that.

"Commander," she said slowly, eyes fixed on the cloth in front of them, "what do you think this ceremony will do to you."

He was quiet for a moment. Too quiet.

"I know what they told me," he said at last. "That it will bind my loyalty more visibly. That it will make my commitment to the crown and the princess unquestionable. That it will remind enemies that our unity is not to be tested."

"Do you believe that is all," she asked.

"No," he said.

She turned her head. His profile was sharp in the low light, every line thrown into relief. His thumb pressed again to the scar at his jaw, the only sign of strain.

"What else do you think it will do," she pressed.

He let out a slow breath. "It will put another chain on me."

The admission landed heavy in the room.

"You accept that," Mira asked.

"What I accept does not change whether the chain exists," he said. "The question is whether it sits where I can carry it, or whether it drags others down as well."

"You should not have to carry so many," she said, surprising herself with the force of it.

He glanced at her, something like faint amusement and resignation mixing in his eyes. "That is not for you to decide."

"It is," she said, almost without thinking. "I am the one weaving this one."

Their eyes met fully then. The air between them felt charged, a delicate line stretched tight.

"You are doing what they instructed," he said quietly. "I do not blame you for that."

"That is the problem," she whispered. "I am not only doing what they instructed."

His brow furrowed, confusion and wary interest flickering across his face. "Explain."

She could not tell him everything. The archives. Selene's bargain. The exact nature of the control. Those truths were too big to spill here. She did not know who might be listening at the keyhole. The walls in palaces had the habit of growing ears.

But she could not stay silent either.

"I have to balance protection and binding," she said. "The channels I sew decide how the ritual flows. They decide what shares and what stays."

"And you are not certain you agree with what they want to share," he said, reading enough without seeing the text.

"No," she said.

His gaze dropped briefly to her bandaged finger. "You injured yourself."

"The cloth did," she said before she could temper it.

He looked sharply at her. She cursed her loose tongue.

"How," he asked.

"It wrapped around me," she said reluctantly. "Too tightly. It drew blood. It accepted it."

He watched her face with that soldier's focus that took everything in. "Why."

"Because I tried to force it away from you," she whispered. "And it refused."

Silence filled the room again. He did not move. Neither did she.

"You are saying the garment is loyal," he said finally.

She gave a faint, humorless smile. "You are used to that, are you not. Loyalty that has teeth."

He considered her. A slight tension appeared at the corner of his mouth, as if he fought the urge to smile back in spite of everything.

"I did not ask it to be loyal," he said.

"I did not intend it," she answered. "That is the worst part. My magic made its own choice."

"You care," he said.

The words were simple. They hit like a blow.

She inhaled sharply. "Do not read more into it than there is."

"No," he said. "I think I will read exactly what is there."

His thumb pressed harder against the scar. It was the only sign that he felt the same electricity hanging between them. His posture remained composed, but his voice was a fraction lower now, more intimate.

"Why are you really distressed," he asked. "Not the polite answer. The true one."

Her throat tightened. The urge to deflect, to change the subject, to make a joke about stubborn cloth pressed at her tongue. She bit it back.

"They want to use this bond to control you," she said quietly. "In ways you have not been told."

He went still. Completely still.

"They told me it was to share pain," he said, each word careful. "To keep us from being careless."

Mira swallowed. "It is that. And more."

"Tell me," he said.

She shook her head. "I cannot. Not without putting both of us in more danger than we already are. But you need to know that this is not just about reminding the kingdom that you are loyal. It is about making sure you can never forget it."

His jaw tightened. His thumb pressed against the scar, then dropped to his side.

"Does this control my thoughts," he asked.

"If I do my work correctly," she answered, "no. But it may give her the ability to tug at the part of you that rises in battle. To dull it or sharpen it. To influence how far you go."

A muscle jumped in his cheek. "So they mean to tie not just my life to the crown, but my strength as well."

"Yes," she whispered.

He looked down at the garment. The silk lay smooth, innocent. The gold stitching glowed faintly. It did not look like something that could chain a person's will. Perhaps that was part of its danger.

"Can you refuse to sew those channels," he asked.

"I can," she said. "If I wish to be replaced. And if I wish someone far less troubled by this to take my place."

His eyes narrowed. "They would bring in another."

"At this stage," she said, "yes. The pattern is almost set. It would not be difficult for a more obedient enchanter to finish it."

He exhaled slowly through his nose. "Then refusing does not free me."

"No," she said.

"Then why are you breaking yourself on this," he asked.

Her temper flared for a second, sharp and surprising. "Because someone should care that your life is being carved into pieces and handed to other people."

It hung there between them, raw and unpolished.

She flushed. Her hand curled into a fist on the table.

He studied her, expression altered by something she could not quite name. The dryness in his eyes lessened. The soldier faded at the edges. A man stepped forward.

"You say that as if my life is worth that care," he said quietly.

"It is," she said at once, before caution could stop her. "Whether you believe that or not."

He held her gaze.

For a moment, neither of them was in the palace. Neither was artisan nor commander. They were just two people at a table with something dangerous between them.

Something shifted. Not loud. Not dramatic. Just a small, undeniable shift.

His eyes dropped briefly to her mouth, then flicked up again. The air felt thinner.

He looked away first, as if breaking the moment before it grew into something neither of them could afford.

"You asked me once if I trusted the crown," he said. "Let me answer the question you have not asked."

She waited.

"How far will I go for the kingdom."

She exhaled slowly. "Yes."

He looked at the garment again, at the careful seams, at the places her magic had sunk in. His hand rested on the table, close enough that she could see the faint calluses on his fingers.

"I have already given it my youth," he said. "My body is marked by it. My sleep is broken by it. My name belongs to songs I do not sing."

His thumb drifted back up to the scar on his jaw and rested there.

"If they tell me that my death will save it," he said, "I will walk to it."

Mira's chest hurt.

He did not stop.

"If they tell me that my will must bend to keep thousands alive," he continued, "I will bend it."

He looked at her then, and the tired sincerity in his eyes almost broke her.

"If they ask me for everything I am," he said, "I will give it."

His next words came softer, like something clawing its way out of him.

"Until nothing remains of me."

The sound of water in the basin ticked once as a droplet fell. Outside, somewhere in the distance, bells marked the hour. Inside the workroom, Mira felt something inside her tear slightly.

"You cannot mean that," she whispered.

"I do," he said.

His thumb pressed against the scar again, harder this time. His eyes did not drop.

"Because if I do not," he said, "then every death under my command, every man I have ordered forward, every village I have walked through after battle, all of it becomes meaningless. This is the bargain I made when I accepted the rank they offered. I do not get to walk away from it because it begins to cost me parts of myself I would have preferred to keep."

Her eyes stung.

"You are not a bargain," she said. "You are a person."

"Some days, I am not sure the difference matters," he replied.

The calmness in his tone cut deeper than anger would have.

She wanted to shake him. She wanted to tell him that no duty was worth annihilation. She wanted to demand that he keep something back, something that belonged only to him.

Instead, she said, very quietly, "There should be a line."

He considered. "Perhaps. But if the choice is between my line and the line of someone who never had a chance to choose anything, I know which one will move."

She stared at him.

"You think your life can pay for everyone else's," she said.

"No," he said. "I think it should pay before theirs does."

That was the moment her resolve cracked.

Not in an obvious way. She did not gasp or sink to the floor. It was more subtle, like a thread snapping deep inside a seam where no one could see. A foundational stitch giving way.

Until now, she had been trying to find a path that did not sacrifice him. She had tried to balance the enchantment, to make it as gentle as a binding of this type could be. She had thought that if she worked carefully enough, she could thread him through this ceremony with minimal damage.

His words made her understand that he had no intention of preserving himself.

He would walk into annihilation if it protected others.

The crown was more than willing to let him.

Her magic hummed in her chest, fierce and desperate.

If he would not save himself, someone had to.

She looked at the garment, at the channels that would soon tie his awakened strength to Selene, giving her the ability to call or quiet the very part of him that made him who he was on the field.

She had intended to temper that bond. To make it bearable. To make it fair.

Now she understood that fairness had nothing to do with what would happen if Selene or the council panicked.

Her careful restraint might leave too much room for them to use his selflessness as fuel until nothing remained.

Duty was already his chain.

Love became hers.

She did not want to call it that. The word felt too big, too dangerous. But whatever lived under her ribs had moved from quiet care into something fiercer when he said he would give everything. It refused to accept that.

She had to move her line, even if he would not move his.

"Commander," she said softly.

He looked at her.

She did something reckless.

She reached out and put her hand over his on the table.

The contact jolted them both. His skin was warm, callused. Her magic surged, racing through the point of contact and into the cloth under their joined hands. The garment pulsed, recognizing the circuit.

His eyes widened just slightly. For once, he did not hide it.

"Mira," he said.

It was the first time he had spoken her name.

She felt the sound of it like a physical touch. Her heart pounded so hard she thought he might hear it.

"You must keep something," she said, words tumbling out in a hush. "There has to be a part of you that is not theirs. Not the kingdom's. Not mine. Not hers. Just yours."

He held her gaze, eyes darker than she had ever seen them.

"If I keep that part," he said, "someone else may lose everything. Can you accept that."

"No," she said. "I cannot."

A faint, almost helpless breath left him. He bowed his head slightly, as if acknowledging a blow and accepting it.

"Then we have reached the place where we disagree," he said.

"Yes," she said. "We have."

She did not let go of his hand.

"How far will you go," he asked then, voice low. "For what you care about."

She looked at him for a long moment.

"Far enough to stand in front of you when they try to take the last pieces," she said.

His thumb moved under her hand, shifting back toward the scar on his jaw. He did not pull away.

"That is unwise," he said quietly.

"I am not here to be wise," she replied. "I am here to sew. If I must choose between sewing you into obedience and sewing you a way out, I know which one my hands will listen to."

His brow furrowed.

"What do you mean," he asked.

She almost told him.

Almost told him that she would not just temper the channels now. She would twist them. She would build in a path that did not lead outward, but inward. A hidden fold. A secret escape.

A loophole in magic.

If someone tried to use the bond to override his will, she could design it to bend around him, to spill harmlessly into shared sensation rather than control. It would be risky. If she misjudged it, the rite could backlash. But if she did nothing, Selene might be handed a perfect lever.

She closed her mouth. She could not say any of that.

"The more they push," she said instead, "the more I will try to keep the enchantment from breaking you."

"Even if it breaks you," he asked.

The question cut deeper than any blade.

She swallowed. "I do not matter as much."

He exhaled sharply, almost a soft curse. His thumb pressed hard against the scar now, as if that pressure kept something inside.

"Do not say that," he whispered.

"It is true," she said.

"It is not," he answered. "You think your life weighs less because the council does not speak your name in their halls. That is not how balance works."

"Balance does not decide who they send to war," she said. "Power does."

"Then we have to build balance ourselves," he said. "In whatever small ways we can."

"You are giving everything," she said. "That is not balance."

His hand shifted under hers. For a moment, she thought he would squeeze it. He stopped himself.

Their hands lay together on the silk, touching through the thin layer of her skin and his calluses. The garment rested under that contact, the enchantment humming quietly, absorbing every unspoken vow.

He looked down at their joined hands, then up at her.

"Do you regret saving me," he asked suddenly.

The question knocked the breath from her lungs.

"You remember," she whispered.

"Not clearly," he said. "Only fragments. A cold tent. Voices arguing. A hand on my chest. Warmth when there should have been nothing."

She wanted to deny it. To keep the distance. To protect them both. The truth pushed through anyway.

"I do not regret it," she said. "Not for a moment."

His eyes softened, just a little.

"Then do not regret what you do now either," he said. "Whatever choice you make with these threads, make it fully. Half measures will ruin us faster than any enemy."

"You trust me with that," she asked.

"No," he said. "I trust that you care."

It was worse.

It was also somehow better.

He finally pulled his hand back, breaking the circuit between them. The garment cooled, the hum settling.

The air felt different without his touch. Emptier and clearer at once.

He straightened, the commander sliding back into place around the man.

"I should leave," he said. "They will notice if I am gone from the upper floors for too long. Suspicion grows quickly in this building."

Mira nodded. Her hand felt cold where his had been.

He hesitated near the door. "Mira."

Again, her name did something to her.

"Yes," she said.

"Whatever they ask of me," he said, "whatever chains they lay, I want you to know something."

He paused, searching for words he was not used to speaking.

"I walk into it with my eyes open," he said. "If I disappear under it, remember that it was my choice."

She shook her head. "They took too much choice from you already."

"Perhaps," he said. "But some of it is still mine."

He opened the door, then looked back once more.

"Do not destroy yourself for my sake," he said. "The kingdom needs more people who see what you see."

She almost laughed. "And fewer who do what you do."

"Perhaps," he said.

He left.

The door closed.

Silence returned, but it was not the same silence.

Mira moved back to the table and rested both hands on the garment. Her pulse roared in her ears. The echo of his words lingered in the air, heavy and unshakable.

Until nothing remains of me.

She could not accept that. She refused to accept it.

Duty was his chain. He had wrapped himself in it willingly, convinced that this was the only way to give meaning to all he had done.

Love became hers.

She did not name it out loud. She did not need to. Her magic already knew. It had known from the night in the tent. It had known when the lace drew her blood. It had known when the garment tightened protectively around him.

She lifted her needle.

Her resolve was no longer to make the enchantment gentle.

Her resolve was to build a secret fault line into the chain.

If they tried to use this bond to strip him of what remained of himself, she would give the magic somewhere else to go. Back into shared feeling, into the weight they chose to carry together, instead of into command.

If it killed her, so be it.

She set her first stitch in the altered pattern, a small, precise deviation that no one who did not understand her magic would notice. It was risky. It was almost foolish.

It was the only answer she had to his words.

With every pass of the needle, she whispered into the cloth, as if the threads could hear.

"You will not take all of him. You can hurt him. You can pull at him. You can share his pain. But there will be a center you cannot reach."

The garment warmed, accepting her intention.

In that small, hidden way, she began to pull her own chain tight.

Not to bind him.

To stand between him and the people who would.

Whether he asked her to or not.

11

The palace looked different on the eve of a wedding.

Servants moved in tighter lines, voices kept low but quick. Lanterns burned longer in the corridors, their light stretched thin along stone. Fresh rushes had been laid in the public halls, and someone had scattered petals in the main stairwell, though Mira suspected they would be crushed into a sorry paste before morning.

From her workroom, she heard the echo of rehearsals rather than saw them. Musicians testing chords in the great hall. A priest's voice rolling through a half spoken litany. The clatter of chairs being arranged and rearranged as stewards argued over view and precedence.

The city outside the palace walls was already celebrating, or bracing, or both. She had heard it in the distance when she woke in her narrow bed that morning. Bells, laughter, the faint thump of drums. A marriage with the Commander at its center meant street vendors would sell whatever they could dress in blue and silver. It also meant soldiers at every gate and an unspoken tension in every crowded room.

Inside her workroom, there was only the dress.

Mira stood in front of it as the light faded, hands at her sides, fingers stiff.

The gown was finished. Perfect. Terrible.

On the outer layers, it was ceremonial attire, not an ordinary dress. Technically it was not a gown at all, but formal battle silk, tailored to fit over armor and under symbolic plates. The lines were clean, sharp at the shoulders, slightly flared toward the knees. Gold thread traced patterns of protection that looked like simple scrollwork to untrained eyes. The collar caught the light in a quiet band.

Inside the seams, her magic waited.

Channels for pain. For shared sensation. For that dangerous link to the part of Kael that woke when death brushed past him. She had done everything she could to blunt their cruelest edges, twisting paths so that control would slip past his mind more often than not. She had built in a hidden fold, a secret loop. A fault line that might misdirect the worst of what Selene or the council could attempt.

It might not be enough.

That thought had followed her all day.

She heard it in Iris's cautious instructions. In the sidelong looks from other servants who knew something important was being prepared behind this door. In the way the gown warmed when she brushed it, as if eager for the ceremony it had been born for.

She heard it most in her memory of Kael's voice.

Until nothing remains of me.

He had said it like a fact, not a threat. Not dramatic. Simply true.

She could not keep sewing toward that.

Mira closed her eyes and listened.

Her magic curled inside her ribs, restless, aware. The bond she had woven into the cloth tugged at her senses. It felt as if the gown were breathing. The channels she had shaped seemed to hum in anticipation of what tomorrow would bring.

She imagined it. The great hall filled with people. Selene in her own ceremonial attire. Kael in this garment, blood pricked onto its surface as the priest spoke. The channels lighting under the skin. The bond flaring to life fully. The council watching, satisfied that their weapon now had a lock built into it.

Her stomach clenched.

There had been moments, earlier, when she had convinced herself that the fault line she had hidden in the enchantment would be enough. That she had found some middle path between obedience and defiance.

The pages in the archive would not leave her alone.

Overridden instincts. Quieted minds. Warriors who died as extensions of someone else's fear.

Mira opened her eyes.

Even if her hidden work held, even if the ritual did not completely control him, the dress still gave them too much. Too many paths. Too many ways to press on a man who already had nothing left he was willing to keep for himself.

The candle near the window flickered as a draft slid through the room. The shadows shook, turning the gown into a pale shape that seemed to lean toward her.

Mira reached for the table.

Her hand closed around the handle of the small blade she kept for cutting heavy thread and reinforced cloth. It was not long, but sharp, with a narrow, slightly curved edge. The metal had been tempered specially, with a bit of silver folded in so it would not warp near enchantments.

She had avoided using it on the gown except when absolutely necessary, because metal carried magic too easily. Today, that was exactly why she needed it.

She held it without lifting it from the table for a long time.

Her heart pounded in her ears. Her breath refused to settle.

If she destroyed the dress, she would destroy weeks of work. Royal work. She would undo the ceremony's central piece. There would not be time to remake something this complex before the wedding, even with a dozen enchanters working through the night. The rite would have to change, or be delayed, or abandoned.

The palace would not forgive that.

They would call it sabotage. Treason.

They might kill her.

Her hand tightened on the knife.

If she did nothing, Kael would walk into that hall tomorrow wearing a chain stitched by her own fingers. He would offer himself up to a ritual that might take the last pieces of himself he could have kept. He would do it willingly, thinking it was only another burden he had to bear.

Love, or whatever stubborn shape her feeling took, refused to accept that.

He was prepared to give the kingdom everything until nothing remained of him.

She was not.

The thought of him looking at her afterwards, quieter, obedient, with some dangerous spark hollowed out of his eyes, made her feel physically ill.

No one else was going to stop this.

Selene would not. The council certainly would not. Iris might sympathize, but even she would not destroy royal work.

That left Mira.

"Forgive me," she whispered to the empty room. She was not sure who she meant.

She lifted the blade.

Her wounded finger throbbed against the handle as she stepped closer to the gown. The silk gleamed softly, catching the last of the light. It looked so harmless.

She reached for the lower hem first. If she cut there, along a key channel, the damage would not be cosmetic. It would be structural. The enchantment would be forced to reroute. With the right cuts, it would fail.

She pressed the tip of the blade against the inner seam, just where a line of magic fed upward toward the heart.

Before she pushed, she closed her eyes briefly and pictured another path.

She could walk out of this room. She could leave the dress

untouched. She could pretend she had never seen the archive passages. She could accept Selene's protection, her advancement, the workshop, the safety.

Kael would still carry the cost.

Her hand moved.

The blade slid into the seam.

The reaction was immediate.

Magic surged up through the metal like a live current. Her hand jolted. Pain shot up her arm, sharp and hot, as if she had thrust the knife into lightning.

Mira gasped and almost dropped the blade. The only thing that kept it in her grip was the death tight curl of her fingers around the hilt.

The gown shuddered.

The silk bucked slightly under the knife, not physically tearing yet, but pulling. The channels she had sewn did not want to be cut. They strained against the blade, trying to guide magic around it, to close the wound.

Mira gritted her teeth and pushed harder.

The blade sliced through the seam, cutting not just fabric but spell-work. The enchantment shrieked in her senses, a soundless cry that reverberated in her skull. The air crackled with static. The candle flame on the table flared, then guttered.

Her magic reacted instinctively, trying to stabilize the rupture. She forced it back. If she let it mend, she would lose any chance of undoing this.

She dragged the knife upward, splitting the channel that ran along the side of the gown. Each inch burned her hand. Magic lashed up into her arm, wild and hot, looking for somewhere to go.

"Stay with me," she hissed, though she did not know whether she spoke to herself or to the spell.

The gown's enchantment fought to preserve itself. Threads tightened. Seams tried to heal. The blade carved through them, tearing apart not just cloth but the connections she had so carefully laid.

Pain blossomed in her chest.

Not her own.

For one heartbeat, she felt something that was not the room, not her body. A flash of disorientation, the sense of someone far above these floors staggering, steadying, looking for the source of a sudden wrench inside his ribs.

Kael.

The bond was not fully sealed, but some of the channels were awake enough that destroying them tugged at the other end.

"I am sorry," she whispered. "Hold on. Please."

She had to work quickly. If the bond alerted anyone sensitive enough to feel it, they might come looking before she finished.

She moved the blade to another seam, cutting across the heart channel this time. Heat slammed into her hand so hard she nearly screamed. The metal glowed faintly along the edge, the silver within it catching and reflecting the surge of energy.

The gown's magic flared in panic.

Light burst from the cut.

Not bright enough to blind, but bright enough to throw sharp shadows across the walls. The air smelled suddenly of metal and something like singed air, without smoke, without fire. Her ears rang.

Her hand began to go numb. She tightened her grip until she felt skin split at her palm. Blood slicked the hilt.

"Keep going," she told herself through her teeth. "Do not stop now."

She slashed downward, across the central front seam, slicing through the bundle of channels that converged there. The gown convulsed.

This time, the magic did not just shoot up her arm. It exploded outward.

Across the palace, lights flickered. Somewhere above, a chandelier chimed against itself as if shaken by an invisible hand. Wards woven into the walls hummed an alarm. Anyone with the slightest sense for magic would feel something crack.

Mira staggered backward, almost dropping the knife at last. The gown swayed on its stand, the silk rippling as though caught in a wind that did not exist.

The enchantment screamed.

Not in sound. In pressure.

It pressed against her mind, a flood of sensation that made it hard to breathe. Pain and confusion and desperate clinging rose from the cloth, searching for an anchor. Without the channels intact, it had nowhere to go.

She slammed her magic into it one last time, but not to heal. To sever.

"Enough," she shouted, though her voice came out rough and small under the roar in her head. "Let go."

She plunged the blade into the seam just below the collar, twisting it as she cut through the last intact path that tied the enchantment together.

The spell snapped.

Energy tore free from the gown in a violent rush. It shot up the blade, seared through her hand, and burst out into the air as a wave of force that knocked her backward.

She hit the floor hard. Her head bounced against stone. Stars burst across her vision. The knife clattered away, skidding under the table.

The gown sagged.

The light that had glowed faintly in its seams winked out, like embers dying under water. For the first time since she had started working on it, Mira felt nothing emanating from the cloth. No hum. No pulse. No warmth.

It was just fabric now. Expensive. Ruined.

Her ears still rang. Her hand burned. Her palm was a mess of blood and half healed skin. The bandage on her finger had torn. A thin line of blood ran down her wrist.

She tried to sit up and nearly fell forward again as the room tilted. She braced herself against the floor, panting.

Outside, in the corridor, voices rose in alarm.

"What was that."

"Did you feel it."

"It came from this side, I swear."

"Check the wards. The wards spiked."

Mira's heart hammered. She forced herself to look at the gown.

The front seam had a jagged tear where she had cut. The slit ran from the collar to the hem, uneven and ugly. The inner layers were shredded. Gold thread hung loose in some places, snapped in others.

She had done it.

The enchantment was gone.

So was her plausible deniability.

A fist struck the door. Hard.

"Seamstress Mira," a voice shouted. "Open in the name of the crown."

She tried to stand. Her legs trembled but held. She slipped in a smear of her own blood near the knife, caught herself on the table, and grabbed a cloth to wipe her hand as quickly as she could.

There was no time to hide what she had done. No time to pretend this was an accident. The magic surge had been too big, too violent, too obvious.

"Seamstress Mira, open immediately," the voice barked again.

She swallowed and forced herself to the door. Her body felt heavy, slower than it should. The knife still lay under the table. She left it, wrapped her hand in the cloth she held, and unlatched the door.

Guards stood outside, four of them this time, not two. Their faces were taut and wary. Iris Merrow hovered behind them, eyes wide, color drained from her cheeks.

"What happened," Iris asked, looking past Mira into the room. "There was a surge. It tripped half the wards on this floor."

Mira's voice wanted to fail. She made it work.

"I was working," she said. "There was a reaction."

One of the guards pushed the door fully open and stepped inside without waiting for permission. His gaze went at once to the gown.

He froze.

"So that is what you call working," he said.

The others followed his stare.

The ruined front of the gown sagged open where she had sliced through it. The tear gaped like a wound. Loose threads dangled. The air in the room still trembled faintly from the aftermath of magic released too fast.

Iris moved forward slowly, as if approaching a body. Her eyes were fixed on the damage.

"Oh," she breathed. "Mira, what have you done."

Mira had no good answer.

The nearest guard turned on her. "Step away from the table," he ordered. "Now."

She obeyed, backing up until her shoulder touched the wall.

Iris tore her gaze from the dress and looked at her, really looked. Her eyes dropped to the cloth wrapped around Mira's hand, saw the blood seeping through. Her jaw tightened.

"This was not a simple mistake," Iris said. Her voice was soft, sorrow and fear mixed. "Was it."

Mira opened her mouth. No sound came at first. She tried again.

"The enchantment was wrong," she whispered. "It would have broken him."

She saw at once that the words were a mistake.

"You speak of the Commander," one guard said sharply. "How would you know what it would do to him. You are a seamstress. Not a council mage."

"I read the texts," she said, feeling the ground shift under her feet. "I saw what the ritual was meant to be. I knew what my stitches would carry. I could not let it happen."

"They sanctioned it," another guard snapped. "You do not decide what is allowed for the crown's protection."

"The crown does not get to hollow him out entirely," she shot back before she could stop herself.

The room chilled.

Iris inhaled sharply.

The lead guard stepped closer, expression hardening. "Listen carefully, Seamstress Mira Nerielle. You are admitting that you knowingly destroyed a royal artifact of great significance, on the night before a ceremony that is meant to secure peace. You did this without permission, without consultation, and in direct opposition to an approved ritual. Do you understand what that sounds like."

"Yes," she said.

"It sounds like sabotage," he said. "Like treason."

The words fell like stones.

Treason.

She had expected it. Hearing it spoken aloud still sent a cold shiver down her spine.

"The kingdom will be at risk if they use a ritual like that," she said softly. "You think I acted against it, but I acted for it."

"No," the guard said. "You acted for him."

She could not really argue.

Iris stepped forward. "Let me speak with her alone. For a moment. She is in shock. We need clarity before we call this treason."

The guard shook his head. "The wards on this floor spiked in a way I have never felt. The council will have sensed it. Maybe the princess herself. There is no time for private talks. We have to secure her now."

The word secure sounded too close to cage.

Two of the guards moved toward Mira. Hands went to sword hilts, not drawn yet, but ready. She made no move to run. Where would she go. She was on an inner floor of the palace, surrounded by stone and steel and eyes.

"Hold out your hands," one guard ordered.

She hesitated, then unwrapped the cloth enough to comply. Her palm was a mess of blood and angry red skin. The bandage around her finger had darkened with fresh staining.

The guard stared. "You did this with a blade."

"Yes," she said.

"You are not a fool," Iris whispered. "You knew this would happen."

Mira met her gaze. "I hoped something else might happen first. That they would listen. That they would see what this ritual truly is."

"People who want something that much rarely listen," Iris said.

Regret shone in her eyes, but it was too late for it to change anything.

The guard took a length of narrow chain from his belt. It gleamed like polished iron, with small sigils etched along its length. It was unmistakably enchanted.

"I am placing you in confinement by order of the crown," he said. "You are to be brought before the council at their next convening and charged with sabotage of a royal artifact, interference with a sanctioned rite, and disobedience of oath."

The words rang in her ears like hammer blows.

He wrapped the chain around her wrists. It hummed as it settled, a low vibrational buzz that sank into her skin. Her magic recoiled. The sigils flared faintly, dampening the hum of her power until it felt like a muted ache instead of a flowing tide.

She felt suddenly small inside her own body. Not empty, but contained.

Iris reached out as if to touch her arm, then withdrew her hand before she made contact. "You should not speak more than necessary when they ask you questions," she said. "You are too honest. That will not help you there."

"Will the ceremony proceed," Mira asked her.

Iris hesitated, glancing at the ruined dress, then at the guards. "They will scramble," she said carefully. "They may try to salvage some kind of rite. I do not know which pieces they will remove or replace. You have changed its shape. That is certain."

Mira exhaled.

It was not relief exactly.

It was something like grim acceptance.

She had torn the threads. She had cut the channels. Whatever ceremony happened now would not be the one Selene and the council had planned.

Love had become rebellion.

Not of singing banners and raised fists, but of a knife taken to a dress in a quiet room.

"Move," the guard said.

Mira walked.

As they led her out of her workroom, she caught a last glimpse of the gown on the table. Its torn front gaped in the lamplight. It looked like a body that had been opened and emptied of something vital.

Her heart twisted. Despite everything, she felt grief. It had been her work. Her craft. Her weeks. Her blood. Destroyed by her own hand.

But underneath that grief, something steadier lived.

She had not let them lace him into a chain he could never break.

There would be consequences. The word treason hung over her like a drawn blade. She might never walk out of this palace freely again.

As she turned the corner, escorted between two armored figures, she felt a faint tug in her chest. Far away, somewhere else, someone reacted to the break in the bond.

Kael.

She hoped he understood.

Even if he did not, even if he raged, even if he never forgave her, she would not undo what she had done.

Better a thousand chains fall on her than one more that swallowed the last of him.

12

The chains around Mira's wrists hummed with quiet pressure. Not sharp pain, not outright suppression. Just a constant reminder that her magic belonged to someone else now. She walked where the guards directed her, down the corridor that led toward the interior holding rooms, her bare feet slipping slightly on polished stone.

Her workroom door closed behind her like a sealed tomb.

Guards flanked her on all sides. Iris walked ahead, pale and tense, fingers curled into her ledger as though she could write her way out of this if someone only let her finish a sentence. She kept glancing back, but she could do nothing now. Her authority ended at paperwork. Mira's fate was no longer an issue of organization. It belonged to power.

They reached a turn in the hall. The passage to the right led to the council chamber, where the king's advisors would gather by morning to judge her. The passage to the left led downward, toward holding rooms. The guards turned her left.

Movement at the far end of the corridor stopped them.

A figure walked toward them. Fast. Too fast for someone casually crossing palace floors. Boots struck stone in deliberate rhythm. It was not a noble's pace, not the drifting stride of someone escorted by servants.

It was the pace of someone who had decided something and did not intend to ask permission.

Mira recognized the gait before she saw the face.

Kael.

He wore his ceremonial jacket half-buttoned, its structured lines sharp against his frame. His hair looked as though he had pushed his hand through it, the strands unsettled. His sleeves were rolled at the forearms, as if he had forgotten protocol in his hurry. His jaw was tight, and his eyes fixed straight ahead as though he had no interest in the guards he was approaching.

He stopped when he reached them.

The guards did not move aside. They stood solid, confused by the presence of a high-ranking officer outside his assigned path. Mira tried not to breathe too quickly, tried not to look like someone waiting for rescue.

"Commander Kael," the guard captain said. "This prisoner is to be taken to confinement. You are interfering with royal procedure."

"I am not interfering," Kael said. His voice was quiet, even. Dangerous. "I am here to hear the charge."

"The council will address that," the guard replied.

"No," Kael said. "I will address it now."

Mira's pulse hammered. She wanted to tell him to stop. To walk away. To let her bear this alone, because her rebellion did not need his ruin. But her voice died in her throat. He ignored the guards and looked at her.

His eyes were not angry. They were searching her face for what he already suspected.

Mira held his gaze.

The guard captain stepped between them. "Commander, this is not your concern."

Kael looked down at the man's hand on his chest and then raised his eyes again, slow enough to make the motion feel like a warning.

"Remove your hand," he said.

"You are not above palace law," the captain snapped.

"No," Kael said. "I am the one who carries it onto battlefields."

He wasn't shouting. He didn't need to.

The captain hesitated. His duty warred with instinct. Instinct lost.

He dropped his hand.

Kael stepped forward, closing the space between Mira and the guards. Not touching her. Not yet. But he stood close enough that the authority he carried wrapped around her like a shield.

"What is she accused of," Kael asked.

His voice remained controlled, but underneath it something shifted. Mira recognized the tone. It was the same one he used when he gave orders that might decide whether men died.

"She destroyed a royal artifact," the guard captain said. "She interfered with a sanctioned ritual. She committed sabotage."

Kael looked at Mira again.

"Is that true," he asked.

He was offering her a moment. A choice between silence and truth.

Her breath trembled as she spoke.

"Yes."

The guards stiffened. Iris closed her eyes as if bracing herself. Mira expected Kael's expression to harden. Instead, he nodded once, quietly.

"Why," he asked.

The question was not accusing. He was giving her a chance to speak before anyone else condemned her.

Mira looked down at the chains, at the red welts they left on her skin. She lifted her eyes to meet his.

"Because it would have taken everything from you," she said.

Gasps rippled through the corridor. Even the guards shifted.

Kael frowned slightly. "Explain."

"I studied the ritual," she said, voice steady despite its softness. "I found the old records. It was not just about shared burden. It would have tied your strength to the crown. Not just your life. Your will. Your instincts. The part of you that keeps you alive."

Kael's jaw tightened, his thumb twitching toward the scar near his jaw before he stopped it mid-motion.

"You knew they did not tell me everything," he said.

"Yes."

"And you destroyed it," he said.

"Yes."

"You risked death," he said.

"Yes."

"For me."

Mira swallowed.

"I would not let the throne take your life twice," she said. "They nearly took it once when you almost died in the war. They would have taken what remained tomorrow."

Silence crashed over the hall.

Iris looked at Mira with something like heartbreak. The guards stared as if they had just discovered that a quiet seamstress might be a threat to the kingdom.

Kael took one long, slow breath. The air felt heavy with it.

Then he lifted his head, eyes sharp, and looked at the guards.

"Remove her chains."

The guard captain blinked. "Commander, you do not have the authority—"

"I do," Kael said, voice still even. "Because you are binding someone who acted to save a royal asset. Me. If her claim is correct, she protected the throne's most valuable tool."

Mira flinched at the word tool. Kael saw it. His voice changed.

"She protected a life," he said, sharper now. "Not property. Not a weapon. A person. And you will not punish that without speaking to me first."

The guards hesitated. Orders warred with fear, protocol with instinct. If they disobeyed him, they risked consequences from the military wing. If they obeyed him, they risked the council's wrath.

They froze.

Iris stepped forward. "Commander Kael speaks truth. According to palace codes, if the ritual threatened a sovereign asset, and someone acted to protect that asset, they must be allowed to speak before confinement is enforced."

The guard captain glared. "This is not protection. This was destruction."

"She destroyed something harmful," Iris said. "That requires hearing, not punishment."

The guard captain looked at Kael, truly looked, and realized he would not win this fight in a corridor.

"Very well," he said through clenched teeth. "She will speak. With a council witness present."

Kael nodded once. "Good. Then we walk."

He stepped behind Mira, close but not touching, a silent statement that he would follow if they tried to pull her away.

They moved down the hall again. Controlled chaos unfolded around them. Servants whispered. Palaces walls hummed with confusion. A steward stumbled out of a side room, stared, stepped aside. Another guard started to ask a question and stopped mid-word when he saw Kael's face.

No alarm sounded. No swords were drawn. But the air felt tight, held together by tension that could snap at any moment.

They reached a small holding chamber meant for questioning before confinement. A council clerk rushed to unlock the door, stammering a greeting and nearly dropping his quill when he saw Kael.

Inside, the room was bare. A table, two chairs, a brazier for warmth. Nothing else.

The guards directed Mira to a seat. Kael stood, not sitting, not leaving, a silent warning that no one would force her alone in this.

The clerk dipped his pen shakily in ink. "State your name."

"Mira Nerielle," she said.

"State your crime."

"I destroyed an enchanted garment meant for the royal ceremony tomorrow."

"State your reason for doing so."

She lifted her chin. "To save Commander Kael."

The quill faltered on the page.

Kael spoke before anyone else could. "Her actions fall under protective intervention. If she is correct about the ritual, she acted to preserve the crown's military strength."

"She is not a recognized scholar," the clerk said weakly. "She cannot interpret ritual text with certainty."

"She can," Kael said. "She saved my life once before. She knows my body better than half the doctors in this building."

The quill nearly dropped again. Mira stared at him. He had never spoken of it to anyone. Her throat tightened.

The clerk swallowed. "Explain."

Kael's expression did not change. "She saved me on the battlefield years ago. I was dying. She used magic without sanction to keep me alive."

Shock rippled through the room.

Mira whispered, "You remember."

"Not clearly," he said. "But enough."

"Why did you not report her then," the clerk demanded.

Kael looked at Mira, then back at the clerk.

"Because she saved my life," he said.

That stopped everything.

Mira felt something break open in her chest. Not pain. Not hope. Something deeper, nameless, frightening.

The clerk stared, realizing the implications. If Kael confirmed an unsanctioned enchanter saved him years ago without reporting her, the council might question him, not just her.

Kael did not waver.

"And I am confirming it now," he said. "She is not a threat to the kingdom. She is the reason its most decorated soldier survived long enough to serve it."

The clerk wet his lips. "Commander, if that is true, then she has been in violation for years. She should have registered or been trained, or—"

"Or imprisoned," Kael finished. "And who would you have sent to the front then. A general half as competent, with a quarter as many victories."

The room went deathly quiet.

Kael stepped closer to the table.

"You owe her," he said. "The kingdom owes her. And if you punish her now for saving it twice, you are fools."

Mira had never heard him speak like that. Not in command. Not in defiance. Not in self-protection. It was the closest thing to fury she had seen from him, controlled like a blade held by the handle.

The clerk swallowed again, sweat forming at his temple. "I will need to write a statement. I must fetch a council representative to hear this."

"Do it," Kael said.

The clerk fled.

The door shut. The guards remained outside. Kael and Mira were alone.

She turned to him. "You should not have said that."

"I said what was true."

"It will cost you," she whispered.

"It already has," he answered.

She stared.

He finally looked at her fully, no guard, no clerk to witness it.

"You destroyed something that would have taken the last piece of me," he said. "You stood alone for it. I will not let you stand alone after."

"It is still treason," she said.

He shook his head. "Then I will be a traitor too."

"No," she said. "You are needed. You cannot choose me over the kingdom."

He took one step closer. His voice softened, but the softness was fiercer than his command tone.

"I am choosing what keeps me alive," he said.

She could not speak.

He reached up and touched his thumb to the scar along his jaw. Not to hide a tremor. To remind himself why he was doing this.

"They would take me apart piece by piece," he said. "So I am taking something back."

The door opened suddenly. Iris burst in, breathless.

"They are gathering early," she said. "The council. Someone sent word of a disruption. They will not let this be a private hearing. They want a verdict tonight."

Kael's jaw set. "Then we leave tonight."

Iris stared. "You cannot. If you flee, you condemn yourself. And her."

"It is already condemned," Kael said. "They want to use me. And punish her for refusing to let them. I am finished being their weapon."

"You cannot outrun the crown," Iris said.

"Then I will not run," Kael said. "I will walk. And she will walk with me."

Mira swallowed. "And then what."

"Then we refuse to be tools," Kael said.

Iris looked between them. Fear, awe, and something like reluctant respect flickered across her face.

She exhaled sharply. "You will need a path no one expects."

She grabbed a ledger from her belt, tore out a map sketch, and shoved it into Kael's hands. "There is a service stair behind the eastern armory. It goes to the lower courtyard. If you move quickly, you will pass before the guard shift changes."

Kael nodded. "Will you turn us in."

"Ask me tomorrow," Iris said. "Right now I do not see you."

Kael reached for Mira's chains.

"Do not touch them," Iris hissed. "They are sealed. You will trigger alarms if you try to break them."

Kael paused. "Then how do we remove them."

"You do not," Iris said. "Not yet. She leaves in them and they are cut later."

Mira's voice cracked. "I cannot go like this. I am bound."

Kael stepped close to her. Close enough that his breath warmed the air between them.

"Then I will carry what you cannot use," he said.

She shook her head. "You cannot fight an entire palace."

"No," he said. "But I can walk through confusion faster than they can reach consensus."

It sounded absurd. It sounded impossible. It sounded like the only chance they had.

Iris cracked the door and peered out. "No one is here. Now. Go."

Kael pulled Mira with him. Not by her chains. By her arm, carefully, fingers gentle around her elbow where the skin was unbruised.

They stepped into the hall. The guards were gone. Summoned to the council room to prepare for the sudden verdict. Controlled chaos worked in their favor. Orders moved too fast for logic.

They passed servants who froze at the sight of them. Some bowed. Some stared in confusion at Mira's chains. None tried to stop them. A steward started to speak and stopped when Kael looked at him. A pair of soldiers opened a door out of reflex as they approached.

They reached the service stair. Its stones were worn smooth from centuries of feet. They descended quickly. At the bottom, an outer door stood ajar. Cold air seeped in, carrying the scent of night and wet leaves.

Mira turned once, looking back into the palace. For a moment, she saw it as she had always feared it could become. A place where loyalty was measured in how much a person was willing to lose.

Kael squeezed her arm gently.

"Look forward," he said.

She did.

They stepped through the doorway together.

The courtyard lay quiet under moonlight, lanterns guttering in the breeze. The stable gate at the far end would be guarded, but they had seconds before anyone realized the guards should not be here.

Kael guided her across the stones. His steps were certain. The chains hummed around her wrists. The world felt both too real and too fragile.

A shout broke across the courtyard.

"There. Stop them."

Mira's breath caught.

Kael did not stop.

They reached the gate as three guards turned toward them. One grabbed for his weapon.

Kael's hand moved only to lift Mira's bound hands slightly, showing them.

"You want to arrest the one who saved your commander's life twice," he said.

It was not a question.

The guards froze. Duty crashed against uncertainty. One lowered his hand from his sword hilt.

The other stepped aside.

Controlled chaos. Confusion moving faster than command.

The third guard swallowed and pushed the gate open.

Kael nodded once. "Thank you."

He led Mira through.

As they crossed the threshold into the dark street beyond the palace, Mira felt the last of her breath finally break free.

They did not run.

They walked.

Together.

For the first time, their bond was not born of accident, desperation, or duty.

It was chosen.

13

They left the palace without running.

Running would have drawn arrows. Walking drew whispers instead. Mira was not sure which felt worse.

Once they crossed out of the main gate and into the outer streets, the city swallowed them in noise and shadows. The night pressed close, damp and cool. The lanterns here were cheaper than the ones inside the palace. Their light flickered more, reaching less far. People moved through narrow alleys with lowered heads, wrapped in cloaks against the mist.

Mira's wrists still burned where the enchanted chain circled them. Every step sent a small jolt through the sigils etched into the metal. Her magic had been pushed down to a thin, aching hum, like a voice trapped behind stone.

Kael walked beside her, close enough that their shoulders nearly brushed. He did not touch her, but his presence steadied her more than any chain could bind. His gaze swept the street, cataloguing exits, corners, clusters of people. Years of war had taught him that danger rarely came from where it announced itself.

They turned off the main road into a narrower lane where cobblestones gave way to packed earth. Dim light seeped from cracks under a shuttered door. Somewhere above, someone laughed sharply, then fell silent.

"Keep your head down," he murmured.

She did.

They walked like that until the palace walls faded behind them and the city thinned. Houses grew smaller. The smell of smoke changed from perfumed wood to rougher fuel. A stray dog watched them from an alley mouth and then darted away.

When they finally stopped, it was in the shadow of an old storage shed near the outskirts, half hidden behind a stack of broken crates. Kael led her into the narrow space between shed and fence. It was barely enough for two people to stand side by side.

Mira leaned against the rough wood and let herself breathe for the first time since the knife split the dress.

"We cannot stay in the city," she said softly. "They will close the gates by dawn."

"We will not be here by dawn," he answered.

His voice was steady. Too steady. She looked at him. The lines around his eyes seemed deeper now, as if the last hours had carved new ones while he was not looking.

"You are bleeding," she said.

She had not noticed it before, distracted by her own pain. Now she saw the dark smear along his left sleeve where blood had soaked into the cloth.

"Just a scrape," he said.

"Give me your arm," she said.

"You are bound," he reminded her. "Your magic is muffled. You cannot work like this."

"I still know how to wrap a cloth," she said. "Give me your arm."

He sighed and extended it.

The cut was not life threatening. A shallow slice along the outer forearm, probably from a brush against an unfiled edge of armor or a careless door latch in the rush. It had clotted, then reopened. The skin around it was red.

She tore a strip from the edge of her own sleeve with her teeth and good hand, ignoring the sting in her palm where the knife handle had split the skin. She wound the fabric around his arm and tied it firmly. The pressure steadied her more than it helped him.

He watched her as she worked, eyes unreadable in the dim light.

"When did you pick that habit up," he asked when she finished.

"Working in the repair room," she said. "Needles slip. Bleeding happens. You learn to wrap quickly."

He gave a faint sound that might have been a laugh. Or a sigh. Or both.

Her wrists pulsed under the chain. She looked down at the metal.

"We need to remove this," she said. "Before they use it to track us."

"They can track these," he asked.

"If the sigils are tied to the palace wards, yes," she said. "Even now, they might feel a tug. Not precise. Enough to know I live."

"That may be a comfort," he said quietly. "To some of them."

She knew he meant Selene. And possibly Iris.

"We cannot risk it," she said.

He nodded. "Can you break it."

"Not like this," she said, lifting her bound hands. "The chain is dampening everything. It is not meant to hold raw power, only to keep it from moving."

"Then I will break it," he said.

"It is enchanted metal," she said. "You cannot simply pull it apart."

"Watch me," he replied.

He took one step back, glanced into the street to ensure they were unobserved, then returned. He held out his hand.

"Give me your wrists," he said.

She hesitated and then placed her bound hands in his.

His fingers closed around the chain. He did not yank. He did not strain visibly. He simply held it, testing its give. The sigils along its length flickered faintly in the gloom, reacting to his touch.

"Careful," she whispered. "If you trigger them, they might flare."

"Good," he said. "Let them."

"Kael," she began.

He tightened his grip.

The chain hummed louder. The sigils brightened. A sharp sensation shot up her arms, like hot water poured over frost.

He changed his angle, braced his foot against the shed wall, and pulled.

The links did not snap. They twisted.

The magic inside the metal reacted to the strain. It flared along the length of the chain, quick and bright. Mira gasped as her magic, muffled for so long, surged up to meet the pressure like water punching through a cracked dam.

For one second, the world narrowed to the heat of his hands on the chain and the rush of power up her arms.

"Pull with me," he said.

"I cannot," she said. "I am bound."

"Not anymore," he replied. "They suppressed you. They did not erase you. Pull."

She took a breath and reached for the thinnest threads of magic she could still feel inside herself. They responded slowly, sluggish, like limbs asleep. She shoved them toward the chain.

The sigils sparked in protest.

Cracks appeared in the etched lines. The magic fizzled, trapped between his brute strength and her directed push.

The chain snapped.

It broke not in the middle, but at the clasp, where a weaker link joined enchanted metal to simple hook. The sound was small and sharp in the tight space.

Mira staggered. Kael caught her by the waist before she could fall.

Her wrists were suddenly weightless. The absence of the chain felt almost dizzying.

Magic rushed back into her like breath after too long underwater. It flooded her chest, her arms, her fingertips, raw and unsettled, as if complaining about being constrained.

She leaned into his hold for a moment, eyes closed.

"Are you hurt," he asked.

"Only everywhere," she said, with a weak attempt at humor.

His hand stayed at her waist longer than necessary. Long enough that awareness of his touch spread through her in a slow, warm wave. She stepped back, gently, and he let her.

He tossed the broken chain into the shadow under the crates. It landed with a muffled clink.

"They will find that," she said.

"Good," he said. "Let them know you are not bound anymore."

"That will not comfort them," she said.

"It will comfort me," he answered.

There was no argument she could make against that.

They walked again, leaving the shed behind. The streets grew quieter as they moved toward the outer edge of the city, where small gardens and narrow lanes gave way to open ground and low, dry walls. A wind picked up, carrying the smell of distant fields.

"Where will we go," she asked.

"North," he said. "There are villages where my name still means something besides orders. We can find shelter. For a while."

"For a while," she repeated.

He did not pretend it would last.

They passed through a small postern gate that led to one of the lesser used roads. No guard challenged them here. The palace had not yet realized where to tighten its nets.

As they walked away from the lights, the sky opened wider above them. Stars pricked through the clouds like hesitant lanterns.

Mira's steps slowed. The rush of escape, of decision, of broken chains and defiance, began to ebb. Left behind it was bone deep exhaustion.

Her legs felt heavier. Her injured hand throbbed in time with her heartbeat. Her magic, newly returned, pulsed unevenly, not yet settled.

Kael noticed. Of course he did.

"We should rest," he said. "You are staggering."

She shook her head. "If we stop now, we will not start again. Not before they find us."

"Then we will not stop far," he said.

They walked until the road dipped into a shallow hollow where an abandoned shepherd's hut leaned against a slope. Its roof sagged, but its walls still stood. A low stone wall circled a patch of ground that might once have held sheep.

Kael pushed the warped door open. It creaked. No one waited inside. Only dust and old straw and the lingering smell of animals.

"It will do," he said.

Mira sank onto an overturned crate and let her shoulders slump. The hut's thin walls muted the wind. It felt like a bubble, fragile and briefly separate from everything beyond.

Her hands rested on her knees. In the faint light from the doorway, she could see the faint glimmer of golden thread dusted along the cuffs of her sleeves.

She frowned.

She brushed at it. The particles did not behave like dust. They clung, warm under her fingers.

In the chaos of destroying the dress and being knocked to the floor, she had not noticed that some threads had fused into her clothes. When the enchantment exploded, pieces of it had scattered. Some of those pieces had chosen her.

She held her sleeve closer to her face. Thin strands of silk and gold were tangled in the fabric, almost invisible unless she looked for them. Her palm, still sore from gripping the knife, tingled as she touched them.

Kael sat on the low ledge opposite her, watching her expression.

"You carried some of it with you," he said.

"It carried itself," she said. "I did not ask for this."

She plucked one thread loose. It stuck to her skin. A faint pulse of magic ran from her finger to her wrist, then to her chest.

Not the full force of the destroyed enchantment. A fragment. A note from a song that had once been whole.

She thought of Selene's original plan. A garment binding Kael's strength to the throne. The risk of control. The danger of that power in the wrong hands.

Then she thought of the cloak draped across her shoulders. Plain wool, travel stained and thin at the edges. No magic. No protection.

Her mind made a leap that frightened her even as it convinced her.

"What are you thinking," Kael asked quietly.

"That the ritual is not dead," she said. "Not entirely. Pieces of it live in these threads. And in me."

He looked at the gold dust clinging to her sleeve. "Can you use that."

"Yes," she said, with growing certainty. "But not as they intended."

"You mean to weave it again," he said. There was a hint of warning in his tone.

"Not as a dress," she said. "Not as something they can put on you and call theirs. As something we choose. For us."

He watched her carefully. "Explain."

She took a breath. Her magic steadied a little, sensing purpose.

"The ritual was always about sharing," she said. "Pain. Strength. Awareness. They wanted to use that sharing to control you. To pull you back when you went too far. To push you when you held back."

"Yes," he said.

"But sharing can be balanced," she said. "If I reweave some of these threads into something smaller, something not tied to the crown, I might be able to preserve the part that keeps us alive without giving anyone else a hand on you. Or on me."

"What would it bind," he asked.

"Not your strength to Selene," she said. "Ours to each other."

He went very still.

She continued, words tumbling now that they had begun.

"Your battle gift woke when you almost died," she said. "Mine woke when I refused to let you. They are connected. Frayed, tangled, but connected. If I take what is left of this enchantment and rework it, I might be able to make something that makes us less breakable. Together."

"How," he asked.

"By sharing strength," she said. "Not pain alone. When one of us weakens, the other's power rises to meet it. Not to override. To keep us moving. To keep us standing."

He stared at her.

"That is dangerous," he said.

"So is everything we have done," she replied. "At least this danger would belong to us."

"If I fall," he said slowly, "you would carry more."

"If I fall," she answered, "you would carry me."

He looked away, just long enough for his thumb to find the scar at his jaw. He pressed it lightly, grounding himself in that small, familiar touch.

"Would this hurt you," he asked. "More than you already are."

"It would strain us both," she said honestly. "It would mean that we cannot recklessly burn ourselves out. If one of us pushes too far, the other will pay part of the cost. That is not light."

"And if both of us push too far," he asked.

"Then we break together," she said.

Silence stretched, thin and fragile.

"Why would you ask for that," he said quietly.

"Because they are going to hunt us," she said. "With soldiers, with trackers, with mages. We will not always be able to fight side by side. There may be moments when one of us is cornered while the other is still free. I do not want either of us to fall because we could not reach each other in time."

He met her gaze again. There was something raw in his eyes now, stripped of command.

"And because you love me," he said.

She felt the words like a physical shock.

She opened her mouth. For once, no lie came.

"Yes," she said.

Just that.

He closed his eyes briefly, as if absorbing the truth, or as if it hurt.

His thumb stayed pressed to his scar.

"And if I say yes to this cloak," he asked, "what happens when they catch us. They will try. They will not stop. Selene will not give up what she almost had."

"Then they will find something they did not make," she said. "A bond they cannot easily sever. A power they cannot direct. It will frighten them. And if we are clever, that fear might be enough to keep them from pushing too hard. They will want us alive."

"They already will," he said. "They need me, and now they know what you are."

"Then we use that," she said.

He was quiet for a long moment. The sound of the wind outside whispered against the hut walls. Somewhere far away, a dog barked and then stopped.

"If we do this," he said at last, "there is no walking backward. No pretending we are separate."

"We stopped being separate the night I saved you," she said. "We were just pretending."

His jaw tightened. Then loosened.

"All right," he said. "Make your cloak."

Her heart lurched.

"Are you sure," she asked.

"No," he said. "But I am sure I trust you. That will have to be enough."

She swallowed hard. "Then give me your cloak."

He shrugged out of it slowly. It was a soldier's cloak, not royal issue. Dark wool, heavy, worn at the edges. It smelled faintly of cold air and steel and smoke.

She spread it across the low crate, smoothing the fabric as best she could.

Her fingers moved of their own accord, seeking thread, needle. She had none of her usual tools. Her satchel was still in the palace workroom. For a moment, panic fluttered.

Then she remembered.

Her palm still tingled where she had gripped the knife. Her magic had always preferred thread as conduit, but it could work with less.

She plucked another golden strand from her sleeve. It clung, unwilling to leave the garment that had caught it. She coaxed it free, murmuring soft apology.

She laid the thread across the cloak and pressed her hand over it, closing her eyes.

The magic inside the strand stirred. It recognized her. It remembered the dress. It remembered him.

"This is not your old work," she whispered to it. "You are not for the throne anymore. You are for us."

She reached inward and found the pathways she had already shaped in the destroyed gown, the fault line she had hidden. They were broken, scattered, but not gone. Her blood still carried traces. Her mind still remembered the pattern.

She did not rebuild it completely. She could not. She did not want to.

She built something smaller.

A loop between two points.

Herself.

Him.

She called up the sensation of his presence, the way the dress had reacted when he entered the workroom. The way the magic had leaned toward him. The way her heart had leaned too, whether she wanted it to or not.

Then she called up herself.

Her hand on his chest in a bloody tent. Her fingers pressed over his pulse. Her stubborn refusal to let him slip away.

She wound those two impressions together in her mind. Her magic followed, twining through the golden thread, binding the two images into a single line.

Strength for weakness. Weakness for strength.

Not to steal. To shift.

Like water from one side of a river to the other when a bank erodes. Enough to keep the flow moving. Enough to keep the river from drying on either side.

She opened her eyes.

The thread glowed faintly against the dark wool.

She began to stitch.

She did not need a needle. Her magic pulled the thread through the fabric, entering on one side and emerging on the other, leaving small, neat marks behind. She stitched in a wide circle, starting at the left shoulder of the cloak, traveling around the back, then across the front.

Her fingers tingled as she worked. Her breath grew shallow. This was not simple reinforcement. This was binding. Even in this smaller form, it demanded something from her.

Halfway through, her vision swam. The edges of the hut blurred.

A hand touched her shoulder lightly.

"Stop," Kael said. "You are shaking."

She realized she was. Her whole body trembled, fine and constant.

She did not stop.

"If I stop now, the circle will remain open," she said. "That is dangerous. The magic will leak."

His hand stayed on her shoulder, grounding her.

"Then I am here," he said. "Take what you need."

She almost told him that was exactly what she was trying to avoid. That she did not want to take from him. That this cloak was meant to share, not drain.

Her magic ignored her.

It reached for him.

He felt it. His breath hitched quietly, just once. Then he steadied.

A warmth spread from his hand into her shoulder, down her arm, into her chest. It was not the warmth of touch. It was the warmth of endurance.

Her fatigue eased slightly. Her mind sharpened. The trembling lessened. She realized, with a jolt, that the cloak was already working, even unfinished.

Her weakness had called. His strength had answered.

She closed the circle with the last of the thread.

The glow along the seam pulsed once, then sank into the fabric. The cloak looked almost unchanged. Only a faint line of gold remained visible, circling the whole garment like a subtle border.

Mira sagged back.

Kael's hand slid from her shoulder to her upper arm, keeping her from slumping off the crate.

"Breathe," he said.

She did.

Her lungs ached. Her head pounded. Her magic buzzed like a hive under her skin, unsettled but alive.

"How do you feel," he asked.

"Like I have been unpicked and stitched again," she said.

He made a short sound that might have been a huff of agreement.

"How do you feel," she asked.

He considered. "Strange. Lighter in the chest. Heavier in the limbs. As if some part of me is standing in two places."

"That is the cloak," she said. "We share more than we did before."

He looked at the garment spread across the crate. "Should I put it on."

"Not yet," she said. "First, we decide something."

"What," he asked.

"What we will tell others," she said. "If they catch us. If anyone asks what this is."

He frowned. "It is a cloak."

"It is more than that," she said. "But if we admit it, they will take it, study it, try to use it. We cannot let them know its full nature."

"That is our lie," he said.

"Yes," she said.

He thought for a moment. "We can say it is a remnant. A broken piece of the original enchantment. Useless without the dress. Sentimental, perhaps, but not powerful."

"They will not fully believe useless," she said. "But broken, yes. Harder to unweave. Harder to risk tampering with."

"And the truth," he asked. "What do we call that."

She looked at him. "We call it ours."

He nodded once.

She lifted the cloak, feeling its new weight. It settled over her arms with surprising ease. The magic within it recognized her touch and quieted.

"Put it on," she said, and her voice shook for a reason that had nothing to do with exhaustion.

He stepped close.

She draped it over his shoulders first. He pulled it around himself, fastening the simple clasp at his throat. For a moment, nothing happened.

Then the seam along the collar warmed.

She felt it.

Her own shoulders tingled, as if a similar weight had settled there. Her back straightened without her choosing it to. Some of her lingering fatigue drained away, replaced by a pulse that matched his heartbeat.

He inhaled.

"Mira," he said quietly.

"Yes."

"This is good work," he said.

She exhaled slowly. Relief and fear tangled in her chest.

There was no going back from this.

Outside, in the dark between fields, a horse's hooves struck the road. The sound was distant but clear. More than one horse. The rhythm of an organized patrol.

Kael moved to the doorway and peered out through the crack in the wood.

"Riders," he said. "From the palace. They are already sweeping the roads."

"They are fast," she muttered.

"They are afraid," he said.

Of him. Of her. Of what they represented together now.

He moved back from the door and reached for her hand.

"Mira," he said. "Listen to me."

She met his gaze.

"Whatever happens now, we decide it," he said. "Not them. Not the ritual. Not the past."

"You still speak of choice as if it is simple," she said.

"It is not simple," he said. "But it is ours."

Her chest tightened.

"Yes," she said. "It is."

The horse sounds grew louder, then faded, moving past. For now, the riders had not found the hut.

For now.

Somewhere behind those riders, in halls she had just fled, a princess would be hearing reports of a surge of magic, a destroyed dress, an escaped commander and a vanished seamstress.

Selene would not sit quietly.

Mira was not there to see it, but she could imagine it clearly.

Selene in the council chamber, gray gown neat despite the late hour, listening while stewards and guards spoke at once about broken wards and missing people. Her face impassive. Her mind already moving three steps ahead.

She would not order Kael killed. His value was too great. Nor would she demand Mira's death. Not yet. Not when the girl's magic had proven powerful enough to reshape a ritual.

"Bring them back," Selene would say. "Alive."

"Alive," a council member might repeat. "Even if they defy us."

"Especially if they defy us," Selene would answer. "Dead tools are useless. And we now know she holds fragments of the working I asked for."

Then the riders would be sent out again. With stricter orders. With clearer purpose.

Mira and Kael sat in the half rotted shepherd's hut, wrapped in borrowed quiet.

"We should move before dawn," Kael said. "Find deeper cover before they tighten the lines."

"Yes," Mira said.

She felt the magic in the cloak settle around them like a new kind of weather. Not purely hers. Not purely his. Something shared. Something chosen.

They were hunted now. By the throne. By fear. By everything they had once served.

They were also bound. Not by a crown's decree. Not by accident.

By love. And by a lie they would have to tell the world again and again.

This is only a cloak. It is broken. It is nothing important.

The truth lay in the way their breaths matched without trying. In the way her strength rose when his dipped, and his steadied hers when she flagged. In the way the magic they shared refused to belong to anyone but them.

The Cloak of Ruin, she thought, not without bitter humor. A ruined dress, a ruined plan, a ruined expectation of obedience.

And maybe, just maybe, the start of something that could not be so easily unraveled.

14

*D*awn came slowly.

A pale, uncertain blush spread across the horizon, touching the clouds as though afraid to commit to morning. The fields beyond the city were wet with dew, dark grass glistening like quiet blades under the first hint of light. From the doorway of the shepherd's hut, Mira watched the color grow, thin and hesitant, as if dawn too were hunted and unsure of its own right to appear.

Kael stood beside her, cloak settled across his shoulders, arms crossed loosely. His posture looked relaxed to anyone who did not know him. She had learned enough to see tension in the slight tilt of his head, in the way his fingers brushed the side of his thigh, as if checking the weight of a weapon that was not there.

He noticed her watching.

"We should move," he said. "The patrol that passed last night will circle back."

She nodded. She had no argument left. Only the ache in her limbs and a faint taste of fear rising at the back of her throat.

They stepped out into the cold morning air, leaving behind nothing but footprints on the dusty floor and a single loose thread of gold tangled in the straw. Kael adjusted the cloak's clasp as they walked toward the open road. The fabric rippled around him, catching light that had not yet warmed the ground. It looked like any cloak a traveler might wear. Only Mira felt its hum where it brushed her magic like a small heartbeat, echoing faintly with Kael's.

They walked without speaking for some time.

Silence felt easier than speech. Words were too fragile. They might break something they could not stitch back together. The road curved around low hills, and the city shrank behind them into a distant silhouette, towers dark against a rising sky. Lanterns along its walls looked like eyes still watching.

"Do you know where we are going," she asked quietly after a while.

Kael looked toward the hills. "There is a camp two days north. A place we used to pass supplies through during the war. Some of the soldiers stationed there were rotated out before the council began changing protocol. If any group opposes the crown quietly, it would be them."

"You trust them," she said.

"I trust that they distrust the throne more than they distrust me," he answered. "For now, that is enough."

The wind picked up, ruffling her hair. She pushed a strand behind her ear, feeling the tug of dried sweat and the grit from the road.

"For now," she repeated.

The phrase lingered between them like a temporary shelter, not a promise.

They kept walking. It became clear quickly that Kael adjusted his pace to hers, though she said nothing about it. He was still injured, she knew. Even the small slice on his arm must throb with movement. Yet he walked as though he owed the road something. As though he could not afford to slow, no matter how heavily the past twenty hours weighed on him.

Her exhaustion made her thoughts loud. Too loud.

"What if no one helps us," she asked suddenly. "What if this camp has changed. What if they see us coming and turn us in. Or worse."

Kael did not answer immediately. He turned his face into the wind, thinking.

"If no one helps us," he said, "then we move on. We find another place. We keep walking until we find somewhere we belong."

"That could take forever," she said.

"Then we take forever," he answered.

She stopped walking. He took three more steps before he realized and turned back to her.

"You speak as though it is simple," she said. "As though walking forever is something a person can do. We are two fugitives. One a soldier stripped of command. One a seamstress who destroyed a royal artifact with magic she was never supposed to have. We are not symbols or heroes. We are two people with no plan beyond the horizon. You say forever like it is a choice."

"It is," he said. "It is the only one we have."

His certainty felt like a weight pressing into her chest.

"You do not know what I have done," she whispered. "You do not know what I risked. You do not know what I stitched into that cloak. You accepted it without knowing."

He stepped closer. She forced herself not to step back.

"Then tell me," he said. "Tell me what frightens you."

She swallowed. Her bandaged hand throbbed. The cut on her palm burned beneath the cloth.

"The cloak will protect us," she said. "But it does not protect us gently. If you fall, I will carry more. If I fall, you will. We cannot afford mistakes. We cannot break. We cannot push too far without dragging the other with us. I made something that binds us to survival, not comfort. It will hurt us before it lets us die. I do not know if we can bear it."

"We can," he said.

"You cannot know that," she said.

"You cannot know that we cannot," he replied.

His calm collided with her panic like ice meeting flame. She felt the cloak hum faintly between them, drawing from her strain and offering some of it to him. She felt his steadiness bolster her own pulse. She tried to fight it, but the cloak would not let her drown alone.

"That is exactly what I mean," she said. "We cannot even argue without affecting each other."

He did not look away. "We have fought alone long enough. We can learn to fight together."

Her breath hitched. She hated how badly she wanted to believe him. How much her heart twisted toward him even now, even here on a road that might lead to a gallows.

"What if I doomed us both," she asked. "Not just our bodies. Our futures. What if this binding traps us in a life we do not fit into. What if we choose wrong and cannot unchoose it."

Kael exhaled slowly. He reached up and pressed his thumb to the scar along his jaw. It was a small gesture, but she had come to recognize what it meant. He felt pressure. Emotion. Questions without answers.

"Mira," he said. "You did not doom me. You stopped others from doing so. If we face ruin now, it is ours to shape. Do you understand. For the first time, what happens to me is not in their hands. It is in mine."

"And mine," she said.

"Yes," he answered. "And that terrifies you."

"Of course it terrifies me," she said. "I am not supposed to hold anyone's fate in my hands. I mend tears. I fix seams. I do not change entire lives."

"You did," he said.

She stared at him, anger and fear and something warmer twisting inside her. Her voice came out softer than she intended.

"You never asked me to save you," she said. "Not then. Not now."

"No," he said. "I did not. But I choose it now. I choose what you chose for me. And I choose you again."

Her heart beat so hard she felt it in her fingertips.

"You cannot say that," she whispered. "Not without knowing what comes next. You cannot promise something you may not be able to keep."

He looked at her as though she were a question he wanted to answer carefully, not quickly.

"I did not promise safety," he said. "I promised choice. If tomorrow tries to take it from me, I will choose you again. And the day after. If we burn for it, then we burn. At least the fire will be ours."

Her knees felt unsteady. The road beneath her feet seemed too small to hold what she felt.

"You speak as though we are invincible," she said.

"No," he said. "I speak as though we are not pawns anymore."

He turned and began walking again, expecting her to follow. And she did. Because trying to stand still now felt harder than moving forward.

They traveled north the rest of the morning. The road grew rougher. Trees thickened along the edges. Birds began to stir in the branches overhead. A river appeared in the distance, silver under a brighter sky. In its reflection, the world looked softer, less sharp. But the current moved fast, carrying everything forward whether it wished to or not.

They crossed the river by a narrow wooden bridge. The boards creaked under their steps, and Mira held her breath until they reached the other side. Kael smiled faintly, as if he knew.

Ahead, the land rose into low hills dotted with wildflowers and tall grasses. The wind blew steadily, cool against their faces. The farther they walked, the more Mira felt the city loosening its grip on her mind. But the fear did not fade. It only changed shape.

By midday, they rested beneath an oak at the top of a small slope. It offered shade, and the ground beneath it was dry and firm. Kael shared what little food he had taken when he left the palace. Hard bread. Dried fruit. A strip of smoked meat wrapped in wax cloth. Mira chewed without tasting, hunger replaced by something she could not name.

"You should sleep," Kael said. "You have not since last night."

"You have not either," she said.

"I am used to fighting without sleep," he said. "You are not."

She gave him a sharp look. "Do not pretend you are not human, Kael."

He raised one brow. "I never said I was not human. I said I am used to it."

"That is the same thing," she said.

"No," he said. "Being used to harm does not make harm less real."

She wanted to argue, but the cloak pulsed faintly, as if agreeing with him. She recognized the sensation now. A nudge. A redistribution of tiredness. If she refused rest, he would begin to feel the weight instead.

She sighed and leaned against the tree trunk.

"All right," she said. "Half an hour. No more."

"If I need you to wake, the cloak will do it," he said.

She blinked. "You trust that."

"It has already steadied us once," he said. "I do not need to trust magic. I only need to trust you."

Her breath caught. She closed her eyes, because looking at him felt too full.

Sleep came faster than she expected. It was not deep. It was not gentle. But it was a reprieve. She dreamed of threads, gold and dark, woven through wind and water, binding nothing and everything with the same stubborn knot.

She woke to the sound of distant hoofbeats.

Kael's hand rested lightly on her shoulder, not shaking her, just there to let her feel his presence. She opened her eyes. His voice was low.

"Riders again. East road."

"How many," she murmured.

"Three," he said. "Moving slow, watching both sides."

"They know we headed north," she said.

"They know we are somewhere," he replied. "We should move."

She stood carefully. Her legs felt steadier than before, though fatigue still tugged at the edges of her awareness. The cloak hummed steadily against Kael's back. The golden seam along the edge of it caught the sunlight briefly as he turned.

They moved off the road and into the fields, taking a route that followed deer paths through the grass. The sound of hoofbeats faded eventually. The calm that followed felt fragile, like something that might shatter if she breathed too deeply.

Kael guided them along a line of scattered trees. The sun climbed, warm but filtered by cloud cover. Mira wiped sweat from her brow, wishing for shade or wind. Her bandaged hand throbbed, a dull reminder of the night she had destroyed the dress.

At last, they reached a ridge where the land dropped away into a wide valley. A cluster of distant figures gathered near what looked like an old fortification—barracks built partly into the hillside, roofed with earth and grass.

"That is where we are headed," Kael said.

"You said these people distrust the crown," she said.

"They distrust being used," he replied.

"That is not the same as wanting to help us," she said.

"No," he said. "But they might choose it."

She let the word hang between them.

Choose.

It had become sharper than fate. Brighter than freedom.

As they descended the slope, Mira looked back one last time toward the city. She could barely see the palace towers now. They were faint shapes against a sky washed clean by wind.

She wondered if Selene stood at a window, watching the road and calculating distances. She wondered if council members whispered about traitors and symbols. She wondered if anyone mourned the loss of a dress meant to control a life.

Kael's voice pulled her back to the present.

"We do not walk into this camp as weapons," he said. "We walk as people who refuse to be used."

"Will they understand that," she asked.

"If not," he said, "then we leave. Together."

She nodded.

They reached the base of the hill. Grass brushed against their legs. The cloak rippled behind him as though tasting the air.

Mira walked beside him, heart pounding with fear and something stubbornly hopeful.

Their future was dangerous. It might break them. It might save them. It would not belong to anyone else.

Kael slowed, just enough for her to catch his eye.

"We will face whatever comes next," he said. "And when the world tries to take something from us, I will choose you again."

She swallowed hard.

"Even if it costs you," she whispered.

"Yes," he said.

"Even if it costs me," she answered.

They kept walking.

Toward a camp that might welcome them or cast them out. Toward a road that might lead to ruin or resistance. Toward a future that was neither safe nor certain, but theirs.

The cloak hummed softly, balancing their steps.

Bright as defiance.

Sharp as love.

They walked into their dangerous hope together.